IF THIS BE NOT LOVE

The Jay and Baby Story

Margie Summers-Gladney

Bloomington, IN Milton Keynes, UK

AuthorHouse™
1663 Liberty Drive, Suite 200
Bloomington, IN 47403
www.authorhouse.com
Phone: 1-800-839-8640

AuthorHouse™ UK Ltd.
500 Avebury Boulevard
Central Milton Keynes, MK9 2BE
www.authorhouse.co.uk
Phone: 08001974150

The story of Jay and Baby is based on actual events.
In some cases, names of people have been altered to protect their privacy.

© *2007 Margie Summers-Gladney. All rights reserved.*

No part of this book may be reproduced, stored in a retrieval system, or transmitted by any means without the written permission of the author.

First published by AuthorHouse 1/9/2007

ISBN: 1-4259-5277-1 (dj)
ISBN: 1-4259-5276-3 (sc)

Library of Congress Control Number: 2006906657

Printed in the United States of America
Bloomington, Indiana

This book is printed on acid-free paper.

Table of Contents

PROLOGUE 1

THE CELEBRATION 4

HARRIS ROOTS 7

BABY AND THE STRONGS 11

BABY, THE ADOLESCENT 16

THE MEETING 19

THE UNTIMELY PROPOSAL 22

WEDDING DAY 26
- Jay
- Baby

FOR BETTER OR FOR WORSE 30

THROUGH THE STORMS 39

SETTING THE BAR 45

HAPPY MEMORIES 49

WHEN DREAMS ARE TOSSED AND BLOWN 55

ON THE ROAD-STEP BY STEP 59

HARD TIMES 64

WHEN THERE IS LOVE 68

MORE FRUITS OF THEIR LABOR 75

THE RETURN 79

BABY 93

EPILOGUE 106

PROLOGUE

Complaining does not suit me, particularly in a life rife with the trappings of abundance. Though this afternoon, I am weary from dragging my sixty-three year old body to work everyday this month. My car functions properly. I eat regular meals and there is $100,000 of equity in this house. Though my credit card bill has swollen to over $8,000 due to recent dental work, I am relieved of nagging discomfort. My husband of twenty years has worked well into his retirement and because of him, I have traversed nearly all the states and have needful health insurance. Both of my children have graduated from elite colleges – one law school – and both have achieved measures of success. My eldest has produced the joy of my heart, my grandson, who is a delightful and exhausting body of constant motion. (I regularly stare and smile at his image on my computer screen). I am blessed, and at church most Sundays, sing hymns with heartfelt gratitude.

Yet there are times when tension in my shoulders, headaches and restlessness betray my contentment. And while I know I am fortunate, I feel so weighted by worry and unrelenting demands. The house must be cleaned; a worn fixture must be purchased; I must earn an additional four hundred dollars this week; my unmarried sons' on-going struggles in co-parenting my grandchildren; my husband is away yet again. Then my warranted gratitude is supplanted by anxiety, frustration, doubt and loneliness.

Often, I seek relief from this grip by tending to and beautifying my home which is a God-given prize after a 26 year career in education in Illinois and its extreme climates. It is my masterpiece where I continue to express my eclectic artistry and in doing so find some peace and contentment. It is a haven for my children and grandchildren, whom I have loved so dearly. It is my sanctuary.

Yet it is inadequate. It cannot accord any lasting peace or joy. It pleases me. I am happy here, but as an old English teacher, I know that the word happiness comes from a root signifying temporary, as can only be the happiness produced by this place or the embellishment thereof. It, as well as most of the trappings surrounding me, does not dispel tension, worry, and anxiety. Even my children and grandchildren and dear sisters are not adequate to unburden the full weight of these unwelcome sensations. Wisdom informs me that true and lasting peace and joy exist in something and somewhere else.

My thoughts often drift to a one year period when my mother and father lived with me. Two of our guilty pleasures, my mother and mine, were watching weekday talk shows and soap operas. We were astonished at the awful and idiotic circumstances in which talk show guests found themselves. We were equally amazed at how willingly and unabashedly they aired their stories to the masses. Astronomical debt, serial marriages, broken families, and drug abuse were but some of the tragedies relayed sometimes in gratuitous detail. Mother and I were captivated, and could only shake our heads, scoff, and sometimes even shamelessly cackle. Ironically, the shows were apt preludes to our soap operas whose characters were often embroiled in similar situations: someone cheating on someone else, someone's illegitimate child seeking revenge. The characters and backdrops of the talk shows and soaps were different, but the stories shared striking similarities, leading us to wonder if the soap writers borrow from the misfortune showcased in talk shows. In any case, the shows were somewhat staples in our daily routine.

Afterward, we would talk about life, real life. Strangely and sadly, we at times found parallels between our television programs and the lives of those close to us. Mother, almost invariably, would attribute shortcomings of people, those near and far, to an absence of God, who to her was the only One capable of supplying a moral center and compass. She would recount earlier episodes in her life where abundance was measured in intangibles – faith, hope, resilience – and not in the trappings of secular success so coveted by the multitude. She was a credible testifier – for she had little in the way of luxury during her life, and her stories, words and admonitions, simple in nature, were uncannily striking and comforting.

One conversation led me to other memories that have occupied me and continue to linger in the recesses of my mind. They are memories that create in me solace from my everyday trials and tribulations. The memories are of stories retold in segments over meals, or even recalled privately for my own consumption. Memories which I repeatedly welcome...

THE CELEBRATION

    My thoughts were of my father as I sat at the head of the beige, stone inlay table that had accompanied my mother and him across many years, cities and homes. The nearby bay window funneled a resplendent yellow and white December sun into the dining area, illuming a mosaic of pictures on the wood-paneled walls and the shelves of the walnut and glass cabinet. A blend of aromas (coffee, grits, eggs and bacon) wafted from the adjoining kitchen where several of his children were preparing breakfast, as they had done for him countless times before. Across from me sat our mother, his "Baby," speaking with a familiar ease, thoughtfulness, and grace on an array of topics: the week's errands, a daughter's recent vacation, the mischief of a grandchild and/or husband. The mood was as bright as the sculpted hoary hair that crowned her beautiful sienna face, the face her husband, our father, wholly adored. For today was a celebration of life and love. Those present were to be the blessed audience.

    Midmorning brought the clatter of dishes and a frenzy of a dozen adults readying themselves in suits, dresses, scarves, and jewelry.

If This Be Not Love

Those finished dressing huddled in low-traffic areas as not to be trampled by the rush of those still accessorizing. Every cranny in the house bustled with activity – particularly the bathrooms where frenetic sisters vied for precious mirror space. Others, many of the men, wisely sought refuge on the front cement porch – undeterred by the crisp winter chill. Yet, the three-bedroom, two-bath ranch home proved more than sufficient, and against amazing odds, all were prepared to leave for the awaited affair on time. Honestly, this was not surprising. My parents' possessions tended to be sufficient, and we children – so many years earlier, had each been prepared on time. As a procession of black vehicles crossed the bay window and drew near to collect family and friends assembled, I recalled my parents' life motto, "God will make a way out of no way."

Our ten car caravan drove slowly along the meandering auburn weather-worn roads. Rows of narrow trees flanking a half-dozen homes and open lands rolled past our windows, evoking a collage of thoughts. How often had Jay raced his cars, Granddad's 1929 Chevrolet to his last, 1992 Buick, down this stretch on his way to town, church or on a joyride? As a young man, how many of his young buddies did he leave in the dust? I could only imagine and smile, for the Jay that I knew, was somewhat of a "hot rod."

The rise of the church steeple paralleled the sense of immensity that marked this sacred occasion. The cars settled amid an ever swelling crowd and those among our caravan lined up, then slowly filed into the sanctuary where my father had served so faithfully, and where he would be faithfully honored. Again words entered my thoughts, "If you honor me, my Father will honor you."

One after another took his place at the lectern offering words of praise to the man, friend, neighbor, Christian, and deacon that he had been throughout his life. He was born September 22, 1915; he died November 28, 1997 at the age of 82. The outpouring of praises to this man, my father, who had lived a life well worth modeling by his seven surviving children and generations to come, was most inspiring. I, as well as many others in attendance, was so proud to have had him in our lives. But none of us could experience the richness and beauty of the life that he had shared with his wife, Baby.

His death was caused by myeloma, cancer of the bone marrow. During his final months, Mother and I were his caretakers. There were hours and hours of getting transfused blood and/or platelets, sometimes as often as five days a week. His most severe pain was experienced on the left side of his head where the cancer had eaten into the bone. He was given both chemotherapy and radiation treatments and throughout all of these treatments, he didn't lose his dry sense of humor, positive attitude, or the ability to take care of his basic personal needs. Doctors and nurses found him to be a very pleasant patient and I found this time spent with Mother and Dad under trying circumstances to be a period of spiritual growth and fulfillment. It was a time to give back, though miniscule in comparison, some of what I had received from them.

As the funeral continued, my thoughts drifted to stories surrounding their life. "Jay" as he was known completed the sixth grade of formal schooling. He did not continue because he was needed to help his father run the farm. He had however stood out as a student. As a sixth grader, he won an oratory contest sponsored by Tuskegee Institute, now known as Tuskegee University, as the representative from Chehaw School, the small country school. Although Washington Public, located within the city, was the school attended by children of professionals, the handsome, tall, articulate, country boy, Jay, was crowned the best speaker.

His limited formal schooling had little impact on his intelligence, knowledge of life, ambition and love for his family and people in general. He was one of five siblings, two sisters and three brothers. His parents, William Macon Harris and Lillie Gordon Harris, had instilled in him the virtues of believing in God, being independent, self-sufficient and living a life as a respected Christian. His father modeled such a life for him.

HARRIS ROOTS

William Macon born August 25, 1885, as a young married man, purchased one hundred acres of land which he cleared with mules, axes, shovels, and the assistance of friends and/or hired help. It was not uncommon to see him working late into moonlit nights. He was aggressive with a very strong back and much determination. He industriously labored, sweated and bled upon this ground with all intentions of forging a fruitful sanctuary that would provide a home for his family for generations to come.

Pine timber reached into the skies and a cornucopia of wild flowers, wild muscadines, persimmon trees and blackberry bushes hued the landscape and provided tasty treats for both man and animals. Streams meandered through the heavily wooded back section where a menagerie of rabbits, squirrels and opossums romped and played.

In February of 1929, the bank seized these grounds. Without further details on this transaction, the family could only speculate. What we do know is that Granddaddy had put too much money as well as labor into this land to lose it. The situation causing the failed payment must have been circumstances far beyond his control.

Perhaps a drought? Poor crop productions? Too much rain? Did the Depression influence the land transaction? Was it something induced by racial inequities during an era fraught with racism? Those who could give us the answer are gone but to this day, I lament and feel a great sense of loss, not just for the land that was taken to satisfy a mere debt of $300.00, but more so, for the great vanguard. My heart aches for him for he had put his all into creating a homeland for his family and had gotten so close to obtaining it, only to suffer the agony of having it snatched away.

In God's providence, Granddaddy married a frugal woman, Lillie Gordon born March 10, 1889, who believed in "squirreling away" for a rainy day. Mama Lillie, unknown to her husband, had enough money saved so that they could assume the mortgage of an eighty acre parcel of land that Granddaddy's mother, Josephine, wanted to sell. Ironically, this parcel abutted the 100 acres that were lost.

Knocked down but not defeated, Granddaddy began again to work the land. To accommodate his family, he built a four-bedroom, each with a wood burning fireplace, home with a long hallway running the length of the house. In the hallway near the parlor sat a console Victrola and family pictures adorned the hall walls. The parlor on the right was a small room containing a sofa and matching arm chair in warm burgundy tones. A large picture of Granddad's mother and sisters hung on the wall. Down the hall on the right was Louise and Marie's bedroom simply furnished with a double bed and chair and Jay's bedroom containing a bed and chair. On the left of the house was a large dining room, Mama Lillie and Granddad's bedroom with a beautiful oak bedroom set featuring a high headboard with dark wood inlays and a foot board with four inch posts; a small kitchen with a wood-burning stove, small table and hutch. The fourth bedroom at the end of the hall was Oscar's. The house had a covered front and back porch. An outhouse sat at the end of the large backyard.

This house was the same house that I enjoyed when I visited my grandparents. I played Chuck Berry's "Up in the Morning and Out to School" daily on the old Victrola when my siblings and I visited them in 1958. The magnificent bedroom set is now gracing my antique room. The original home place was well maintained and stood the test of time. My grandparents lived as well as died in this dwelling located at Route One, Box 258, Tuskegee, Alabama.

It was in this house and on this land that my father and his siblings grew up, played the same Victrola, learned Bible verses and developed a philosophy of life that would shape their destiny. I imagine my father's dry sense of humor originated while swinging too high in the swing on the front porch of the house, or while wrestling with his brother, Oscar, and/or teasing his sisters, Louise and Marie, during lazy afternoons between chores. The chores and the toiling in fields, coupled with the expected high level of the performance shaped Jay's work ethics. He would later in life be acknowledged by several of his employers as one of their best and most conscientious workers.

With the aide of his sons, Oscar and Jay, and hired help, Granddaddy planted cotton, corn, sugar cane, white, red, and sweet potatoes, peas, several varieties of beans, peanuts, peppers and other garden vegetables. Several pecan, peach and apple trees were planted. Hogs, cows and chickens were raised to provide meats. Granddad's hunting provided various game.

Throughout the day, while tending to one task or another, Granddaddy modeled the value of "putting in a good day's work, working to have your own, being dependable and having a mindset of using whatever God has given you to your advantage." Other lessons of humility, service, obedience and faith were reinforced while attending Midway Baptist Church where Granddaddy was a co-founder. Jay watched as his father handmade pews for the church, served as a Sunday school teacher and a deacon. These experiences left a lasting imprint on him. He would as an adult find himself emulating many of his father's practices.

Jay was the oldest of Mama Lillie and Granddaddy's five children. Mama Lillie had son, Jimmy Whitlow, prior to marrying my grandfather. He was a dashingly handsome young man and a womanizer who died at the age of forty from a stab wound inflicted by an enraged woman. Son Macon, Granddad and Mama Lillie's second son, died from influenza at the age of six.

Jay was the apple of his mother's eye. He, more than any of his siblings, put into practice what had been taught. His mother found his positive attitude, his humble demeanor, and his respectful manners to be unsurpassed. He was the only one of their children who did not ever "talk back" to her. He was also the neatest of the children and Mama Lillie would use his room to entertain guests when the parlor was in disarray.

BABY AND THE STRONGS

    Unknown to Jay, the future love of his life, Baby, born January 12, 1918 to Willie Lue Freeman Strong and George Washington Strong, was living just five miles away. The majority of her older siblings was married and had left the three-bedroom home. She was the youngest of the twelve children. They were Daisy Lue, David Lee (Buddy), Mary, Garrison, Lenora, Johnnie Mae, Georgia, Nellie Pink, William (Shorty), Emma Lee (Lee) and Jimmie Lois, (better known as Baby). One baby boy died at infancy.
    At the age of three, Baby's eagerness and love for reading and learning were surfacing. She oftentimes asked her mother to read the Bible to her. The Bible and dictionary were two books that were always in her home. While out walking, she would pick up scraps of paper and attempt to read the print on them. She would then demand of anyone in her presence to read the printed material to her. She also begged her mom daily to allow her to go to school with her sisters.
    During the school term, the two teachers of the school stayed with the family during the week and went home on the weekends. Mrs. Coprich was Baby's favorite. She told Mama Strong that it

would be okay if Baby came to school and sat in her premier class which was at Clintonville School, a fourth of a mile from the house. Mama Strong eventually allowed Baby to go. Baby loved attending school and learned the materials as quickly as her older classmates; nevertheless, Baby was three and had a tendency from time to time to miss her mother. When the teacher would find Baby crying, she would ask her, "What's the matter? Why are you crying?

"I miss my momma." The teacher would tell Baby that she could go home. Baby would walk back home and be so happy to find her mother safe and sound. On some occasions, she would return to school later in the day.

It was during this time that a raging storm swept through the community. The light rays of the sun disappeared slowly as large black clouds gathered and hung menacingly in the sky. As the storm continued to develop and the winds began to howl, all outside activities stopped and the family took refuge inside the house and sat together quietly.

The house had three bedrooms and a front porch. The front bedroom served as the guest room and doubled as a sitting room. It contained a bed, fireplace, wash stand and basin, and two chairs. The two windows made it a cheerful room as the light streamed through. The second bedroom was Mama and Papa Strong's. It too had a fireplace with a bed, closet and chiffonier. Baby shared her bedroom which contained three beds with Lee, Nellie and Shorty. The dining room was furnished with a long table surrounded with chairs on one side and a high bench on the other side for the children. The kitchen was a favorite place with its wood burning stove, a small table and a hutch that stored the dishes. In the corner and behind the door between the kitchen and dining room were storage shelves for foods. Pots and pans hung over the stove. It was in this house that Baby had always felt safe and secure until this storm.

As the howling winds gathered momentum, the sky darkened. Monstrous looking black clouds hung overhead as thunder roared and lightening bolts lit the sky. The winds whipped around and underneath the house that sat on pillars. It creaked and the windows rattled. Baby sat, nestled snugly in her mom's lap. To Baby, the storm was never ending.

where to be seen when he came home. Mama Strong told him what she was doing. Sadden by his baby's response to the whipping; he vowed that he would never whip her again.

Capitalizing on Baby's status as the baby, her older siblings used her to get permission to attend community affairs that they felt would not get an immediate approval. They knew that it was harder for Papa Strong to say no to her than to the rest of them. Baby would get the permission, but once granted each knew the rule to be followed. "Be home before sunset."

He was a deacon at Shiloh Baptist Church and served as a Sunday school teacher and treasurer of the church for many years. His resignation from the church treasurer position in later years was due to his progressive hearing loss.

Papa Strong, along with the children, farmed the land and tended the livestock. They planted cotton, corn, sugar cane, millet, sweet, red and white potatoes. The garden was filled with greens: collards, cabbage, mustard, turnip; beans: lima, pole and string; onions, shallots, okra, peppers and tomatoes completed the assortment of garden foods. Cows, mules, hogs, chickens, dogs and cats roamed over the land. Because Papa Strong's favorite pastime was fishing, the family enjoyed many meals of fresh fish.

After harvest, syrup making, killing and smoking a hog, Papa Strong would travel to Georgia and work making ties for railroad tracks throughout the winter.

BABY, THE ADOLESCENT

Shorty, Lee and Baby, the three youngest, could have easily been named "The Three Musketeers" for their inclination to venture into daredevil activities. It was nothing for them to climb trees to unprecedented heights, explore the deep woods filled with rattle snakes, water moccasins, stinging bees, wasps, poison ivy, poison oaks and many thorny plants.

The water streams and/or water holes found in the woods were dangerous because of unpredictable depths of the water as well as the inhabitants living in them and should have been off limits; however, there were no off limits where these three were concerned. Exploring the streams at their deepest point was the challenge. Lee, who declared herself the caretaker of Baby, oftentimes made many trial "leaps" to test the difficulty. If she found an activity to be too difficult, or dangerous, she would not allow "Toot," her name for Baby to attempt the feat.

There were also the raids on the watermelon and cantaloupe patch which they knew if caught was a punishable offense. Such knowledge did not deter them. They found the warm, juicy sweet melons irresistible temptations. Their excursions into the patch were invariably discovered because the three would leave behind rinds or uneaten melons that were not to their liking, but more revealing were their tracks. Adolescent reasoning led them to think that maybe deer or some other animal would be blamed as the culprits.

Their beautiful countryside provided other culinary treats which included pears, peaches, plums, and sugar cane. They enjoyed munching on freshly dug up sweet potatoes, chewing the juice from sugar cane, and turning their mouths blue eating blackberries. Fall, when canning was done and syrup was made from the millet and sugar cane, was one of their favorite times.

Baby's adventures however were not without a few hair rising episodes. Three miles from home at an abandoned, vacant house, Lee and she decided to look for left behind treasures. That was however, before Lee looked through an opened window and saw or "thought she saw" a big black bear. Grabbing Toot's hand, she tore away from the house in terror of being pursued and mauled to death. That was the end of exploring old, abandoned houses.

Deeply etched in Baby's memory was the devilish chase by "Junior," a nephew and son of older sister Lenora when she was eleven. Nellie came upon a snake while hoeing cotton with Baby and Junior. She, although older, was too afraid to kill the snake and called to Baby to come and kill it. Baby was brave and killed the snake with her hoe. Bravery took flight however, when Junior picked up the dead snake by its tail and attempted to put it on her.

Petrified, Baby took off running and ran wildly through the field to get away from him, but he pursued her relentlessly. Fear and exhaustion caused her heart to thunder and her chest felt as if it were going to explode. Breathless and sobbing profusely, Baby finally stopped, sat down and yelled, "I'm gonna tell momma! I'm gonna tell momma!"

It was only then that Nellie made Junior put the snake down. Nellie was fortunate for Baby did not tell of the incident when she got home, because if she had, Nellie would have been punished; however, years later after they were grown, she said to Nellie, "You know. You are the only person I have ever hated. Why didn't you stop Junior from chasing me with that snake?"

Nellie responded, "Lois, I couldn't figure out how you could be afraid of a dead snake when you weren't afraid to kill a live one."

What she had failed to understand was that even though Baby was afraid of the snake, she had enough courage to kill it.

Later in life Baby found herself in several situations in which she opted to kill snakes. However, she began to realize that she had a phobia about any snake, be it harmless or poisonous, coming into her living quarters. If this would occur, she vowed that she would not sleep there again.

After entering school, Baby's passion for learning increased. Math and history were her favorite subjects. She repeatedly read her textbooks, above and beyond the given assignments because she wanted to learn as much as she could as quickly as possible so that she could become a math teacher. She would have six glorious years.

Her formal education would end unfortunately after three months in the seventh grade because Lenora, who was a nurse for a white family, and with whom she was living in Tuskegee, moved to Opelika, Alabama. Baby had to move back home where there were no buses or any other means of getting to Lewis Adams School.

Although Papa Strong had allowed her to live with Aunt Lenora and attend Lewis Adams School, he refused requests from two out of state family members who were willing to keep Baby and put her through school. The first invitation came from an older brother and his wife who lived in Chicago and the second came from a cousin, who was a preacher, and his wife who lived in West Virginia. Papa Strong's response to them was, "I can't let my baby leave us."

THE MEETING

    It had been the beginning of Baby's seventh grade year when Jay's sister Louise met her and went home and told him about the girl who was smart in math, talked very well, and had a baby face with long curly hair. Jay decided then that he definitely wanted to meet this girl with the baby face. This decision was the beginning of Jay and Baby, a couple whose relationship would span more than six decades, and whose lives would not only touch but positively impact, as well as ease, the struggles of many.

    He was anxious to meet her; however, this meeting would be delayed because Jay was led to believe that Spence, the brother of Benny, who was Lee's boyfriend, was courting Baby. Spence was indeed interested in Baby but discovered fairly quickly that Baby was not interested in him given the fact that she gave little attention to him and had chosen to see another boy at the time.

    Benny, observing Baby's behavior around Spence, concluded that his brother was not going to get anywhere with her. He then convinced Jay that he should accompany him on one of his visits to see Lee. Jay agreed and finally got his chance to be introduced to

Baby and her family. For him, she was the girl of his dreams. For her, he was a charming, handsome boy for whom she would gladly dump the boy she was seeing.

After meeting Baby, Jay had eyes and time for her only. According to him, "It was love at first sight." There was no need to look farther. Other girls aggressively pursued him, especially Chastity; however, Jay was not interested. Not giving up, Chastity would make a last bold attempt to get his attention and win him over.

Sundays, families attended Sunday school and church, but Sundays were also a day for socializing for the community. It was a time for catching up on old times, sharing news of current events and speculating about the future for the older crowd. For the younger group, it was a time for meeting, greeting, and seeking potential mates.

Baby, as well as her siblings, was brought up to understand that church services were priorities and that socializing took place after church not before. Upon arriving at church, the family would go immediately into the building.

On a Sunday that Jay attended Baby's church, Chastity made her move. With Baby inside, she had lingered outside talking with friends. Jay arrived and she quickly approached him and began to talk and continued talking as she accompanied him into the church. This gave her the golden opportunity and delight of sitting with him during the service. After service, they exited the church building before Baby and her family.

Once outside, Chastity continued her quest while utilizing all of her feminine wiles to entice him. Jay, knowing Baby would be coming out of the church soon, was only half attentive, half listening, and did not attempt to hide the fact that he was watching and waiting for Baby. Upon seeing Baby exit the building, he abruptly dismissed Chastity and hastened to her. Chastity left in mid-sentence and with mouth agape, stood embarrassed and green with envy.

By winter of 1934, Jay had known Baby for over a year and during this time just two of their dates had taken place away from her home. One was a visit accompanied by Lee and Benny to see an older sister, and the other was a walk to a church concert accompanied by a neighbor. In both cases Baby had to be home before nine o'clock.

Initially, Jay made quite an impression on Baby's parents and he had continued to do so throughout the year. When visiting Baby, he always made a point of spending a portion of his time talking with her parents. This pleased them as well as Lee who was delighted by this gesture, for it gave her more time to spend with her boyfriend Benny.

THE UNTIMELY PROPOSAL

Jay, having decided that he was ready to marry, made it known to all of his friends that he had found the girl that he wanted to make his wife. Her parents, who had had many conversations with him, were also aware of his feelings and intent. To them, a forthcoming marriage was inevitable. It was simply a matter of time.

Baby knew of Jay's feelings and intent as well and was flattered by all the attention; but she was hoping that when he did ask to marry her that her father's answer would be "No. She is too young. She is going to finish school." Despite the fact that she had left school because of the move back home, she had not accepted the fact that provisions were not going to be made somehow, someway for her to get back to school. She was still hoping and holding on to this dream.

It was the first Tuesday of the year 1935 when Jay decided that he was ready to ask for Baby's hand in marriage. Neither his father nor mother had met either Baby or her parents. The only information they had received was from Louise's description of Baby and Jay's statement that he had met the girl that he wanted to marry. He invited

If This Be Not Love

his father to accompany him to the Strongs. Jay wanted to show Papa and Mama Strong that he had his parents' support as well as have the two fathers, who were both deacons, to finally meet.

After arriving and following the usual formalities, Jay was told that Baby was away visiting her sister Lee. Jay then informed Papa and Mama Strong of his reason for the visit with his father. He had come to ask permission to marry Baby.

Jay was well liked by Baby's parents so he was given permission and their blessings, but received a stern directive. "Take care of our Baby. You are never to hit her. We have raised her, so if you find that you can't get along, bring her back home." Jay assured them that he loved Baby very much and that he would indeed take good care of her. He was then told to pick Baby up from Lee's and bring her home the following day.

Having obtained permission to marry his dream girl, Jay then happily drove back home and told his mother. Later that day, she went to Lee's house in order to meet Baby and tell her what had transpired.

During this flurry of activity, Baby, at Lee's who is now married to Benny, was totally unaware that decisions had been made that would keep her dream of completing her education from becoming a reality and defer her dream of travel.

Watching Mama Lillie approach the house, Baby could not fathom what was so important as to merit a call from Jay's mother. The greetings were cordial and brief before Baby received news of the recent events. Listening attentively, Baby felt her world crumbling around her. Little did her future mother-in-law know that her insides felt as if they were tied in knots. Mama Lillie ended the visit by telling Baby, "Your Papa told Jay to pick you up tomorrow and bring you home." She then left.

As she watched the car drive away, a menagerie of emotions possessed Baby. She screamed, "How dare he go behind my back and ask Papa before talking to me? Why didn't Papa say, 'No. She's too young.' Papa knows how much I want to go to school. I'm not ready to get married! I don't want to get married now! How dare they? How dare they?"

In an attempt to calm Baby, Lee responded, "Toot, calm down. Calm down. Jay is a great guy. He loves you and you know Mama and Papa both like him a lot. I think he's a great catch."

Baby listened as Lee talked. She knew that Jay was a great guy and she cared a great deal for him but the fact remained that she had other priorities and was nowhere near ready to get married.

The following day, Wednesday, Baby again watched as Jay arrived in his father's 1929 green Chevrolet that glistened from far away. She was ready and overtly appeared fine but was still struggling with what was happening. She was subdued and said little.

On the ride back home, Jay filled with satisfaction and excitement from the past events and looking forward to the future with Baby, declared his love. "I love you Baby and I'm looking forward to you being my wife. I'll take care of you and we'll have a wonderful life together. Will you marry me?"

A deafening silence permeated the air. Baby, looking down and wringing her hands as they lay in lap responded in a strained voice, "I don't want to marry you."

Those words struck Jay as if they were lightening bolts and made such a devastating impact that his feet came off the gas pedal and the car began to slow. "Whaaat did you say?" Dazed, his face took on a look of disbelief and confusion. "You don't want to marry me?"

Seeing his reaction frightened Baby, who was very timid and bashful as a teenager and tended to have difficulty expressing her true feelings, especially to her father. She was now alone with Jay and his face was filled with discontentment. She was without the accustomed protection of her large family. As the car continued to slow down, a sudden, inexplicable rush of fear gripped her.

She had known Jay to be the epitome of gentleness and kindness, yet at this moment and time, her imagination ran amok. She envisioned being violently attacked or being thrown from the car. Imagining that one or both of these things could happen to her, Baby decided to recant her statement. She would do what was necessary to clear the air. With a wry smile and in the best voice that she could muster, she cooed, "Oh. I was just teasing you. Just teasing." Baby was not teasing.

If This Be Not Love

Jay smiled and slowly regained his composure as they continued the trip to her home. Upon her arrival she found that Papa Strong was waiting for her. He immediately went over what Baby already knew but with one enormous addition. Papa Strong told her that Jay had set the date for the marriage. She would be married on Saturday, January 5, three days hence.

In the meanwhile, Jay and Granddaddy would go to the court house to get the license. He was told that because Baby was underage, her parent's signature was required. Jay then went to pick up Papa Strong. Upon hearing what had happened, Baby wished so much that "I could have told my father not to sign." She couldn't. Papa Strong went with Jay, completed the necessary paperwork and the license was issued.

WEDDING DAY

Jay

A brilliant sunrise ushered in Saturday, the 5th of January, 1935, yet paled to Jay's overflowing sense of anticipation. He tended to his regular chores of feeding the hogs and chickens, milking the cows, and putting them out to pasture. When he had finished, he drew from the well water that he heated on their wood burning stove. He then brought in the tin tub used for washing clothes as well as for bathing.

While bathing, with a smile that radiated complete happiness and joy, he whistled "Here Comes the Bride." He had laid out his clothing on his neatly made bed. His blue suit had been pressed. His white shirt had been starched and ironed. He had selected his favorite tie with paisley design and blue socks. His shoes were polished to a high gloss shine. He wanted to look his very best.

He was very methodical in dressing. He wanted to be a dashing groom for his bride. When he had finished, he looked into the small mirror that hung on the wall, then around the room to make certain that everything was in place, for this would be the room to which he would bring his bride. Once finished with dressing and the room, he paced while awaiting his parents. It had been agreed that he would take Granddad and Mama Lillie to the house of the family's minister, drop them off, then go and pick up Baby and her parents. The marriage was scheduled for 2 P.M.

Baby

Baby rose to the same brilliant sun. It was a lovely day, her wedding day; however, unlike Jay, Baby was facing a day with feelings of trepidation. The day's event had come too soon on her "to do" list. She was neither psychologically nor emotionally ready and her head was filled with questions. What if Lenora had not moved to Opelika and I could have remained in school? Would Papa have been so willing to marry me off? What are my now eighth grade classmates studying? Who took my number one spot in the math class?

She made her bed and pulled on an old dress, then made her way to the kitchen. She would fire up the stove and cook the last breakfast for her parents as an assigned chore.

Throwing on a jacket, she headed for the hen house to gather some eggs. She quickly retrieved several and returned to the kitchen. Biscuits, grits, ham and eggs were prepared. In addition to the coffee pot, a kettle filled with water was placed on the stove so that it could heat for her bath later.

Mama and Papa Strong joined Baby in the kitchen shortly before the eggs were cooked. When everything was ready, Baby prepared their plates, then her own and joined them at the small kitchen table. Conversation was light as they consumed the meal. Baby was subdued. Papa Strong reminded them that Jay would be picking the family up around 1:30 P.M.

With breakfast over, Baby washed the dishes then prepared for her bath in her room. She brought in the tin tub and placed it near the corner of the room. After mixing enough cold water to the boiling water to get it to a comfortable temperature, she stepped into the tub. The temperature of the room caused her to hasten the bath and as she stepped from the tub, she looked at the white satin wedding dress that lay upon her bed.

Unlike her sisters, her dress had not been made by Mama Strong. There was not enough time. It had been given to her by a neighbor. A neighbor's daughter had recently married and moved to Birmingham and she had gone to ask if she could buy the dress. To her surprise and dismay, the new bride's mother told her that she could have the dress. After getting the dress home and trying it on, Baby was astonished. It was a perfect fit. The white satin dress had an empire neck, fitted bodice and long sleeves accented with six pearl buttons at the bottom and to the side of each sleeve. The skirt draped softly to the ankle. Baby liked the dress.

Before putting it on, she would style her long, naturally wavy hair that Jay adored. As most females, what she had, she did not especially like. She preferred to straighten, and then hot curl her hair which is what she did. Having finished her hair and in the absence of wearing make up, Baby put on her wedding dress and looked into the mirror at the finished product. What Baby saw was not the pretty young lady reflected in the mirror. "I never thought that I looked liked anything. People would often tell me that I looked good or nice, but I could never see it." So the pretty girl in her white satin wedding dress who looked back at her "looked just okay but nothing special."

Jay arrived at the agreed upon time and upon seeing Baby, his face beamed and an appreciative smile engulfed his face. After giving her a kiss, he looked lovingly at his bride-to-be as adoration, love and promises of providing for her spilled from his heart. "Enough of that now, let's get going," came the voice of Papa Strong.

The marriage took place as scheduled with both sets of parents and the minister's wife in attendance. The in-laws talked briefly after the ceremony before the newlyweds took Mama and Papa Strong back home. Baby would retrieve her few belongings and Jay and she then returned to get his parents before going to their home.

Louise, Jay's sister, had prepared dinner. It was a typical dinner of collard greens with okra, baked sweet potatoes, fried chicken, and cornbread. Dessert was a peach cobbler. Conversation around the table ranged from issues having to do with the farm to questions to Baby so the family could get to know her. Following dinner, Baby helped Louise clean the kitchen and later joined Jay on the front porch swing where they would end the day swinging and watching the beautiful full moon as it illumined their surroundings.

FOR BETTER OR FOR WORSE

During the first five months of their marriage, both helped with the chores on the farm. Jay also cut wood to make railroad ties to earn extra money. It did not take long before Baby discovered that she was not liked by her mother-in-law. She had not consciously done anything that would offend or disrespect her; however, she slowly came to realize that Mama Lillie was jealous of and resented the love and treatment that she received from Jay. This became crystal clear to her on the day that she was approached by Mama Lillie who wanted to know, "Uh, Umm Daughter Lois. If Jay had a nickel and you needed it and I needed it, who do you think he would give it to, you or me?"

Baby found it unsettling to be asked such a question and hesitated before responding. "Well Mama Lillie, the Bible says that 'a man shall leave his father and mother, and shall cleave unto his wife and they shall be one flesh.' I am his wife and he's supposed to give it to me."

"**Well, I'm his mother! I had him!**"

If This Be Not Love

Through the years, not even the births of her grandchildren softened her attitude towards Baby.

By June of 1935, Granddad, with Jay and a carpenter had built a two-room house, bedroom and kitchen, for the newlyweds. Although small, it was a place to call their own and sorely needed because of the tension between Mama Lillie and Baby. The young couple had been allowed to use a few acres around the house to plant a garden and cotton; however, this privilege did not come without a price. Half of their profits made from selling the cotton had to be given to Granddad and Mama Lillie. In addition, monies advanced for farming and living expenses during the growing season had to be repaid. In spite of the situation, Jay and Baby made ends meet. Their garden provided plenty of vegetables and potatoes and Baby canned many of the items from the garden to have food through the winter.

The end of 1935 was highlighted by the birth of Edward who was born on December 16th. He was a healthy, bouncy baby boy delivered by a midwife. In keeping with the traditions of the time, Baby remained indoors for at least six weeks recovering from the birth as she breast fed the baby and became accustomed to being a mother. She would begin a routine that would span nineteen years of childbearing, learning and then from experiences, changing her approach in parenting, as she incorporated the sage advice that had been given to her by her mother.

Three of the directives tended to stand out in her memory. The first "Spare not the rod and spoil the child." The second "When disciplining your children, you look them directly in the eyes and tell them what you want. Do not take your eyes off of them until they do what it is you want because they will be watching you to see if you are watching them." The third "Do not rearrange your home for a child. Teach that child to adapt to his surroundings. Teach him what he's allowed or not allowed to do." Baby would diligently adhere to these three principles and later pass them on to her children.

With the baby in tow, Baby resumed her daily chores. In addition to cooking and cleaning, she now had a baby and diapers to keep clean. She was fortunate that his birth had come at a time when she was not needed to help in the fields or garden. She would have at least three months before planting time.

Two years later on November 3, 1937, Willie George was born. He was more of a challenge for Baby and Jay for he was very fretful. In an attempt to quiet him, the young parents would walk with him days as well as nights. Not long after his birth, they discovered that his discomfort was due to an inguinal hernia.

He was taken to the doctor who, through agonizing screams of the baby, pushed his intestine that had gone down into his testicles back in place. "The screams from my baby tore at my soul," Baby said.

Upon completing his treatment, the doctor informed Jay and Baby that what he did was only a temporary solution and that Willie would need an operation to correct his condition. Relieved to just get her baby back in her arms, Baby cuddled him as Jay drove home, both hoping that the baby would indeed find relief after such a painful experience.

Somewhat later, they informed Mama Lillie and Granddad of the doctor's statement. Mama Lillie responded, "I don't believe in operations. That baby will die. If you have him operated on and he dies, I do not want to see either of you again."

Being young and not knowing what to do under the circumstances, they decided to refuse the surgery but soon realized that Willie's condition needed some type of treatment. Jay was informed about a truss which he bought for the baby. It aided in holding the intestine in place and Willie did find relief.

In December of that year, Jay along with his brother-in-law Benny, Lee's husband, needing employment for the winter, decided to go to Chicago. It was decided that Baby and the two babies would stay with Mama and Papa Strong.

By February, Jay lonesome and missing his wife and children, wrote and asked her to join him in Chicago. Aunt Lenora, feeling that the cold weather was too severe for Baby to come having so recently given birth, advised her to wait until the weather was warmer. She waited until April. In the meantime, Jay had not found a good paying job and found himself working in a restaurant as a dishwasher.

Fall of 1938, discontentment and disappointment in the work situation had set in although Jay did not talk to Baby about his feelings. He continued to work various jobs but the earnings barely took care of their basic needs. It was only after Baby found a letter written and addressed to Mama Lillie asking her to send money so that he and his family could come back home did she realize the situation. Jay had not mailed the letter. Baby did.

Jay received the money to go home; however, Baby, after finding out their house had been rented out by Granddad and Mama Lillie, and not wanting to return to her in-laws' house, sat and spoke of her feelings to Jay. After the discussion, Jay understood how she felt. He loved his mother but he knew that she had not treated his wife as she should have. He also knew that it was impossible for them to return to their small home because it had been rented. They then decided that Baby would remain in Chicago with her sister Lenora and find a job while Jay and the two babies return to his mother's house.

Although Jay had not taken care of the babies alone for any extended period of time, he without hesitating, willingly accepted the challenge of full time caretaker for their two year old, and ten month old baby. His two sisters and mother would be around for some support, but he fully intended and did take care of his babies the majority of the time.

For six months Baby worked as a babysitter for a Jewish family and corresponded with Jay frequently. It was difficult for her being away from her husband and babies, especially during the Christmas season. As she walked through the neighborhood where she worked, she saw for the first time a toy train winding around its track and her heart ached. She wanted so much to have enough money to buy a train for her baby boys.

Baby continued to work and save money until her return to Tuskegee in early spring 1939. With their house still occupied with renters, Baby, determined not to subject herself to the wiles of her mother-in-law, stayed with her sister Lee for a short time before Jay and she rented a house in Rosenwall Heights, a community not far away. Jay found various jobs to sustain the family.

By 1941, the young couple having experienced an assortment of living arrangements and conditions, found themselves in the Midway community. The Second World War was in progress and Jay was able to get a job helping to build Tuskegee Airport. There he earned enough money to buy his first car, a three year old Ford. While in

Midway, I, Margie, their first daughter was born on February 19, 1942. Baby was delighted to have her first daughter. I would be the first of six daughters.

Shortly after my birth, Baby had a dream and said, "God showed me in that dream my ugly ways." Baby was referring to her treatment of Jay. She knew that she had a good husband and could easily speak of his many qualities to friends and family. "Harris," the name she called him, was often lauded as a great provider, husband and father. He was attentive, had an "easy going" personality and was very loving. Nonetheless, none of these things had eased nor dulled the ongoing pain that she experienced for having been denied schooling. She had admitted to herself that he was not the reason that she was not in school, yet letting go of her dream had not happened.

She had not been an ideal wife during the seven previous years of marriage primarily because she had and at this time still resented that she was not in school. In response to this, Baby became a "pouting wife." There had been many occasions on which she "refused to talk to Harris or respond to him talking to me." As unkind as it may have been, she would ignore him. Baby also at times had a spirited personality and if the occasion called for it, a stinging tongue.

After having the dream, Baby realized that she had to change her ways. The dream was God's way of showing her just how ugly her behavior relative to her husband had been and that there was a great need to change. She did not want to lose Harris nor ruin her family. She resolved that she would count her blessings and strive to be a better wife and person.

This dream would be only the first of several that Baby would have and interpret as God, through the Holy Spirit, communicating with her.

At twenty-four years of age, with three children, Baby had her hands full; yet, she continued to find that her life was made more difficult by the actions of Mama Lillie. While in Midway she began to notice that one of the neighbors, Miss Betty, that she knew well would walk past as she sat on the front porch or worked in the front

If This Be Not Love

yard. To avoid speaking to her, she would turn the umbrella so that it would block Baby out. This behavior hurt and confused her. She didn't understand why or what could have happened to cause Miss Betty to act in this manner.

It was Mama Lillie who enlightened her on the way to the watermelon patch one day after Jay and she had gone down to his parents to get some watermelons. The watermelon patch was across the branch, a wooded area in the back of the land that had a running stream of water. As the two men walked ahead, the women followed. "Uh, Uh hum. Daughter Lois, Mrs. Betty says that she's gonna get you cause you are going with her husband and she told me that you'd better watch out cause she's gonna be carrying a knife."

Taken aback Baby responded, "Mama Lillie, I'm not going with anybody's husband and she'd better know what she's doing." Baby still did not know why or how Miss Betty could possibly accuse her of going with her husband. "Where did this come from and what would I want with her old man?"

Miss Betty continued to walk past and not speak for the duration of the time Jay and Baby lived in Midway.

Occasionally, Jay would ride to work with a neighbor. One day Baby, with Edward on the running board holding on to the driver's door and Willie on the other side holding on, attempted to drive the car in the yard. The major problem was that she did not know how to use the clutch. As she attempted to go forward, the car jerked and stopped, jerked and stopped. Edward having watched her several times letting the clutch up too fast finally said to her, "No, no, Mutt Dear. Let it up slow."

To her amazement, his advice was good and she was successful in getting the car to move smoothly. With a smile, Baby told of her six year old having watched his father and knew how the clutch should be released. She credited him with helping her learn to drive.

Granddad and Mama Lillie wanted to pay off the mortgage on their land that they had purchased from Granddad's mother, Josephine Harris, and they made a proposition to Jay. "You and Daughter Lois can come back to your house. It is now empty. If you pay us three hundred dollars, we will give you the deeds to the twenty acre parcel of land next to our land." The acreage included the land where their house was built.

It was located on Route 65, five miles from Tuskegee University, the place where Booker T. Washington discovered the many uses of the peanut and ten miles from the city that is known for the famous Tuskegee Airmen. It was a combination of cleared acreage and timberland measuring about a quarter of a mile wide and a mile and a half deep. Jay and Baby accepted the proposal.

Although, Jay's pay was relatively small, the young couple had been wise enough to save some of what he had earned and with their small savings; they were able to pay cash for the land. It would be their first major purchase and their homeland for the next sixty years. As we children discovered, it provided not only our primary livelihood, but, timber, wild game and berries, and an assortment of Native American artifacts.

A few months after moving back into their house in 1943, Jay received notice from the army that he was to report to Fort Benning in Georgia. Baby was pregnant with their fourth child and had no idea how she and the children would make it without her husband. He reported to the bus depot which was the pick-up station for draftees. During the interview he was asked how many children did he have. He answered, "Three and one on the way." He was told that the army was not enlisting anyone who had more than two children.

Jay returned home and Baby was elated. They could now get on with their lives. Although the house was small, Jay, Baby, their two boys and baby girl had shelter and land now which was their own. It was a great feeling of accomplishment.

Baby had continued to work at improving her attitude and ways. Over the years, she had grown to love her husband and found herself loving him more and more as they built their life together. She had found that they worked well together and that they were able to sit and discuss whatever situation that faced them. Together they planned and made decisions. Making a decision or acting on a family issue without consulting the other was never entertained. Together they worked to earn their living and together they made decisions on when and how to spend their money. The beauty of the relationship was that there was no "mine or yours." It was always "ours."

If This Be Not Love

She asked Jay one day, "Harris, on the fifth of January, we would have been married eight years. Of all the years that we've been married, which ones were the best ones?"

"Baby, you've been so sweet lately. These last two years you've been as sweet as a grasshopper in a pie jacket." That was one of his funny sayings. Baby smiled.

Baby wanting to find out how he felt about the years when she had acted so ugly asked, "Well Harris? What about the other years?"

"Baby, you really wanna know. You really wanna know the truth?"

"Yes, tell me."

"The other years, your pouting and not talking to me made life really hard sometimes."

"Well Harris? Why didn't you leave me?"

"Baby, I knew you were the baby of your family and that you were spoiled, so I just prayed to God that you would change."

Baby smiled knowing that she had been blessed with an exceptional husband who was wise far beyond his years.

This story always touched my heart and set the bar for me as to true love. Jay, though young, prayed, was tolerant, and willing to wait for a positive change in his wife while continuing to be respectful, supportive and loving. His love for Baby and his family overshadowed the discomfort that he had to undergo. He took his vows to heart when he said, "for better or for worse" and his actions were living proof. I have invariably found myself reciting my favorite Shakespearean sonnet # 116 whenever I think of this period of time in his life and have used line thirteen to format the title of this book..

Let me not to the marriage of true minds
Admit impediments. **Love is not love**
Which alters when it alteration finds,
Or bends with the remover to remove:
O, no! it is an ever fixed mark,
That looks on tempests and is never shaken;
It is the star to every wandering bark,
Whose worth's unknown, although his height be taken.
Love's not Time's fool, though rosy lips and cheeks

Within his bending sickle's compass come;
Love alters not with his brief hours and weeks,
But bears it out even to the edge of doom.
If this be error, and upon me prov'd,
I never writ, nor no man ever lov'd.

Baby's relationship with Granddad was good; however, he did find fault with her after nine years of being married because she had not moved her church membership to Midway Baptist Church. He approached her one day and said, "Daughter Lois, a wife is supposed to be a member of her husband's church."

Baby had chosen to continue attending her family's church as well as Midway. She was finding it really difficult to leave her church. It would take another two years after Granddad talked to her before she could move her membership. In the following years, she and Jay continued to visit her church as well as other churches and participated in church revivals throughout the community.

THROUGH THE STORMS

Baby, walking home from town, had to pass by Miss Betty's house. She and her daughter were sitting out on their porch. Although Baby was still perplexed and hurt by Miss Betty's "umbrella stunt," she was determined to be friendly and spoke to them. In return Miss Betty spoke and invited her to sit and rest a while. During the conversation Baby told Miss Betty how hurt she had been over the treatment she had received from her while living in Midway.

"Lois, Miss Harris told me that you were going with my husband and that I'd better be careful because you carried a knife around on you."

"Miss Betty, how could you believe something like that when you know that Mama Lillie doesn't like me?"

"Lois, at the time Jeff was not bringing home the amount of money that I knew he should have been bringing home. I figured he was giving it to you. With you being her daughter-in-law, I just didn't believe that she would tell that kind of lie on you. It was not until Jeff had the house enlarged and furnished and paid for it all in cash did I realize that he'd been saving the money without me knowing to surprise me. I'm so sorry."

Both Miss Betty and she realized that the knife story was also a lie told to both of them.

Baby stayed a while longer and left. As she made her way home, she felt anger, frustration and hurt at Mama Lillie's attempt to ruin her marriage and her reputation. Mama Lillie's behavior towards her had not changed but maligning her in the community was not only embarrassing but very hurtful. She was the mother of three children, soon to be four, and was trying very hard to improve as a wife and person.

Jay was caught in the middle of a possessive mom that he loved and the wife that he not only loved but adored. Baby would tell him of incidents as they occurred; however, she never knew how he handled them with his mother. She was wise enough to know that he would not be able to stop his mother's antics short of leaving her.

The young couple farmed the land. Both put in as much time as possible in tending the crops. On days that Baby worked in the field, the children would play in the yard. She would leave the field early to go and prepare dinner. Baby loved vegetables and believed in having a vegetable with the majority of her meals. She had realized early in marriage while living with her in-laws that Jay would forego any food in order to eat buttermilk and cornbread. She had watched and had seen how this diet had adversely affected his stomach.

After working in the field, Baby stopped along the way to the house to pick blackberries for a pie. She then made a special effort to prepare a good dinner. As she was finishing the meal, Baby spotted Jay returning from Mama Lillie's house where he had gone to return the mule that they had borrowed. He had with him a bucket. Baby knew exactly what was in the bucket, old buttermilk. Buttermilk didn't get too old for Jay. He would pour it over cornbread or drink it after it had long turned sour and bubbly. She immediately poured the fresh water that she had from the bucket into pans until the bucket was empty.

When Jay arrived she asked him to get some fresh water from the well. While he was gone, she poured the old sour milk into the "slop" for the hogs. After doing it, she became a bit nervous not having done anything like this before and not knowing how Jay would react. Jay returned and washed for dinner. Baby prepared his plate.

"Baby, I bought some buttermilk from Momma's."

"Harris, that milk was too sour and I poured it in the slop."

"Aw!!! Baby you shouldn't have done that!"

"Harris, that milk was sour and not good for you. You need to eat food, some vegetables. I have cooked a good dinner and you need to eat it."

Jay ate dinner without the sour milk or further protest.

He continued to have his cornbread and buttermilk at Mama Lillie's from time to time, but finally realized that it was indeed the source of his stomach problems. He then thanked Baby for caring about his health.

"Baby, you are a good wife. Some women wouldn't have cared what I ate."

Baby however did not on an occasion take such precaution when it came to eating one of her favorite vegetables. It was customary for farmers to put soda around collard greens in late August to keep them thriving into fall. Baby had a craving for collard greens and although she knew that it was too soon to eat the collards after fertilization, she gathered, cleaned, washed and began cooking them anyway. Each time she would open the pot to stir, she said that the spirit would say, "Just as poison as a green snake." Her response was, "I'm going to eat them. My stomach can digest rocks."

When the greens were done, Baby ate until she was satisfied. She would not allow the children to eat the greens and told them that she did not want their daddy telling her that she killed his kids by feeding them poisonous collards. Upon finishing her meal, she got up, walked outside and the greens came spewing up from her stomach. Baby recalled that she never felt sick or had any other side effect from eating the poisonous greens. She felt that this was a time that God not only communicated to her of an impending danger that she ignored, but saved her from herself. It served to strengthen her faith that she did have a heavenly father who looked out for her.

June 24, 1944, Diane, the fourth child and second daughter was born. A living room and a second bedroom were added to the house. Jay and Baby had managed to be the first in the community to get a pump put into their well to provide running water. In addition, they bought a much needed Maytag automatic washing machine. We continued to hang the clothes out to dry.

More pigs and a cow were purchased and they had the calf that was produced slaughtered, butchered and put into a deep freezer in town. Corn was taken to the mill and ground into cornmeal. Sweet potatoes were stored in a potato bank made of stray, mud and corn stalks to protect them from the weather and frost. Peanuts were pulled up and hung to dry and Baby canned fruits and vegetables for the winter months. Jay continued finding various jobs after the crops were harvested. He worked at Tuskegee University doing various labor jobs which he would continue to do for several years.

Over the next five and a half years, farming continued. Jay and Baby contented themselves with raising their children, going to church and making ends meet. They had neither the time nor the money to have much of a social life other than visiting family and friends occasionally. Their quest to provide for the children above and beyond bare necessities came in the form of a console piano bought for me. Piano lessons were given to all of us as long as there was an interest. Baby did not attempt to force any of us to continue once interest had faded.

In addition, I was allowed to take a dance class. Tap dancing lessons were being offered by the school and I wanted to participate. I loved the dance sessions and was having a wonderful time with my dance group. The lessons were abruptly ended when Granddad learned of them. "No granddaughter of mine is going to take dance lessons. That's nothing but the work of the devil." There was no question as to his objection being the last word. The termination of this activity would linger as one of the few events in my adolescence that hurt me deeply.

Jay and Baby had their friends that they saw mostly on a weekend or at church.

One friend, Nathan, lived just off the road on Granddad's adjoining land. He and his wife had two children. His wife Marie suffered from severe arthritis and Baby would visit to help her out occasionally. They became good friends. Nathan was a womanizer and Marie evidently left him; however, he remained in the house and a friend to Jay and Baby.

Nathan extended an invitation to them to go with his girlfriend and him to Montgomery one Saturday for a short getaway. When Saturday arrived, Jay had to work but it was agreed that Baby could go to enjoy the ride. She needed to get out. Nathan picked Baby up and then headed to his friend's house to pick her up. Baby felt comfortable going to Montgomery with Nathan and his girlfriend, even though on one occasion he told her that she was a pretty woman with long pretty hair and that he would ask her to be his girlfriend if she weren't married to Jay. Baby retorted, "But I am married to Harris." That was the end of that. He behaved appropriately thereafter.

Shortly after returning from the trip, Baby got a visit from the neighbor who was about her age and who lived on the adjacent farm. She had just come from Mama Lillie's and had to pass the house to get home. The two had been visiting each other over a period of time and Baby was happy to have her stop by until she said in a rather catty manner, "Lois, Miss Lillie told me that you are going with Nathan."

Apparently, Mama Lillie had seen Baby in the car with Nathan.

Infuriated, Baby responded, "That's a lie! I don't want that man. I have a husband and happily married. I'm tired of that woman lying on me. I'm sick and tired of it!" Her feelings of outrage with her mother-in-law exploded.

After the neighbor left, Baby took off to confront her. She had reached her limit of toleration. Upon arriving, Baby speaking in a voice filled with anger and frustration yelled, "You told Anne Mae that I'm going with Nathan!" That's a story and you know it. (Baby wanted to say a lie but couldn't out of respect) Mama Lillie, I'm sick and tired of you telling stories on me! I'm tired of you trying to ruin my marriage!" I'm tired of it!" Realizing that she needed to stop before she had gone too far, she abruptly turned and left.

Granddad had gone uptown and when he returned Mama Lillie immediately told him of Baby's angry attack and added that Baby had scared her. Later in the day Papa Strong would pass Granddad on his way to visit Baby. He was informed of Baby's visit to Mama Lillie as well.

When he arrived at Baby's, he let her know that he had been told of the incident. Baby looked at her father and this time she could tell him some of what she felt. "Papa, Mama Lillie does not like me for some reason. (She did not tell him that she was jealous of Jay's love for her) and she is telling stories on me to people in the community." She keeps trying to break up my marriage and I'm so tired of it!" He listened to his baby and knew that she was in a tough situation in which he could do very little to help, if anything.

When Aunt Lenora came from Chicago to visit, Baby told her what had been happening with Mama Lillie. Aunt Lenora listened sympathetically and responded. "Lois. Why don't you and the children come to Chicago and live with me? You don't have to put up with her and this treatment."

"Lenora, I'm not going to leave my husband. That's exactly what she wants. She wants to break us up but she's not going to succeed. We love each other and it will never happen."

The family increased by two. Earl was born March 6, 1946 and Linda was born two years later on February 25, 1948. The routine remained basically the same. With just two bedrooms, the children had to sleep in pairs. In the bedroom with the fireplace, which was also the gathering room, Edward and Willie slept in one bed and Diane and I in the other. Jay and Baby slept in the second bedroom. They set up a cot for little Earl in their room. After Linda was born, the two babies stayed in the bedroom and they moved into the living room.

SETTING THE BAR

Baby was set in her ways when it came to annual spring cleanings. It was a time to scrub everything as well as air anything that could not be washed. Mattresses packed with raw cotton were put outside to sun for the day. Because the house sat on pillars and trash and chicken droppings would collect, the entire area underneath the house had to be swept clean as well as the yards around the house.

Spring cleaning also meant that we had to "get a good cleaning out." This meant that it was castor oil time and one of our worst events that happened during our childhood. Baby would heat the oil and the house would reek of its awful smell. She would pour the warm castor oil into a small cup and add a drop of turpentine "to keep the castor oil from griping our stomachs too much." We would hold our noses and dared not gag for fear of having to do it all over again. Those were indeed "ugh times."

Jay and Baby in April of 1950 decided to travel north again so that he could get a construction job in Gary. Mama and Papa Strong agreed to keep the three older children, Edward fourteen, Willie twelve and me eight so that we could finish the school year. They took with them Diane five, Earl four and Linda two. After arriving in Gary, they rented a room. The owner was kind enough to set up an additional bed for the children. This would be home for three months. Jay was blessed and got a job working at a construction company with good pay.

The opportunity to live with Mama Strong provided a fantastic experience for me. Tea time was our very special time. She would make tea or coffee for herself then pour hot water into my light jade cup. Into the hot water, she would put a teaspoon of sugar. If too hot, I could pour some of the water into the jade saucer to cool. At eight, I was in heaven drinking my hot water tea with my beautiful grandmother.

In late June Baby and the three children would go to Chicago. The children stayed with Aunt Nellie and she stayed with Aunt Lenora in preparation to deliver her seventh child. On July 10, 1950, Deborah was born. She was the first of my siblings born in a hospital and in a state other than Alabama. Jay continued to work in Gary and visited Baby and the children as often as he could.

The last of August the entire family returned to Tuskegee to our four-room home. Jay went to work for Sharpe Gravel Company as a truck driver. Edward and Willie prepared to be bused to Lewis Adams Elementary School, a first through eighth grade school in the city, and Diane and I prepared to walk to Chehaw Elementary School, the same school Jay had attended, located a couple of miles from our house. It was a two-room white school building staffed by two teachers and a principal. I had attended the previous year with Willie.

Our farm was located five miles from Tuskegee University Campus off the main highway. Edward and Willie had to walk about two city blocks to get to the road for the school bus pick up. On the other hand, Diane and I had to walk through neighboring farm land, and follow a path through a wooded, swampy area that passed over a stream of water. Children in the Midway community were expected to attend Chehaw for grades one through six.

Baby was not happy with her two little girls having to make this trek everyday in all kinds of weather. It was impossible for us to be taken or picked up from school. Determined that something could be done to rectify the situation, she went to the supervisor of school bus transportation who was the husband of the principal of Chehaw. She was told that no exceptions or special privileges could be granted to her for us.

Refusing to accept his decision, Baby informed him that she would take her request to the superintendent of schools. She did and was granted permission. To assure that there would be no problems from the principal of Lewis Adams, the receiving school, Baby requested that she be given a written document stating the decision of the superintendent. It was prepared and she had won one of many battles that she would encounter in raising her children.

Baby was determined that her children would take advantage of every opportunity that was available to them. They would not fall victims to others or be denied if there was anything she could do about it. Later in the school term, she discovered that the refusal from the bus supervisor was an attempt to keep the enrollment up in his wife's school.

Shortly before starting school, Diane began to complain of different aches. One of her first painful experiences involved her knee. She was in pain and wanted Baby to rub it. At the time Baby was bathing Deborah and told her to allow me to rub her knee. She responded, "I don't want Margie to rub my knee. I want you."

Before Baby could finish, she heard a loud cry from Diane. "OOH God, Stop my knee from hurting. Jesus, stop my knee from hurting!" Diane was six years old. When Baby got to her ready to rub the knee, Diane told her that it didn't hurt anymore. She never complained of knee pain again. There were however, other symptoms and pains to follow and her feet would begin to swell.

Diane and I were often dressed similarly, if not exactly alike. We began the school year with three new dresses each. We would wear one dress for two days then change to another. It was very important to come home after school and take off our school clothes and hang them up. Baby was diligent in keeping our shoulder length or longer hair pretty and decorated with coordinating ribbons. She took pride in having her girls, as well as the boys, going to school looking clean and neat.

Because everyone in the community generally shopped in the same stores, and because the "Nathan incident" neighbor, Anne Mae, would duplicate everything Baby bought for her children, Baby would order clothing from catalogs so that her kids would have somethings that were different.

One of my fondest memories is of the Christmas outfits that were made for Diane and me. Baby had talked with Anna Mae and shared that she was having outfits made, what materials and colors. It just so happened that when buying the materials, she changed her mind on colors. Upon arriving at church in our much more colorful outfits, we found our neighbor's daughter in the original drab colors that Baby had originally planned to buy. Diane and I felt that our outfits were so much prettier.

Her expression of not wanting her children to wear used clothing was another area in which Mama Lillie found fault. Baby was extremely fearful of her children contacting germs or diseases and opted for less things that were new rather than more things that were used.

Mama Lillie, on returning from town, told Baby that there was a yard sale that had some pretty girl dresses very cheap. Then in a very sarcastic tone she said, "Oh, but you don't want your children to wear used clothes do you?"

Even though Mama Lillie could have easily bought items for us, she never did and the fact that she mentioned the yard sale was just another way to jab at Baby. It simply afforded her another opportunity to show her disapproval. Throughout the coming years, she did not buy anything for my siblings and me.

There was no allowance, but we were given money to buy milk to go with our home packed lunch while in Chehaw and sometimes a nickel over that would buy five lollipops or five Tootsie Rolls, or a Sugar Daddy candy bar that was shared. When we got to Lewis Adams School, money was given to buy hot lunches.

HAPPY MEMORIES

During this time, we were happy children. We had fun playing simple games. Diane and I jumped rope, played such games as Little Sally Walters, London Bridges, Here We go Round the Mulberry Bush, Ring around the Roses, Hide and Seek and Hail Over. E.D. and Willie loved to shoot marbles, go fishing, and rabbit hunting. They played softball and went swimming in what was called "the branch." The boys also loved to play checkers and the girls played Jacks and Pick up Sticks. Baby oftentimes competed with Diane and me in Jacks. On occasions when Baby was not in the field during the day, she would listen to "Stella Dallas" and "Young Widow Brown."

Some evenings after chores and homework, family entertainment would include listening to the radio. "Dragnet" was a family favorite. Jay, who was not a big eater, would snack on his parched peanuts and maybe a glass of Kool Aid. Baby would munch on broken pieces of her foot long peppermint stick as she paired it with whichever nuts were available. (peanuts, pecans, brazil nuts, walnuts) She had and to this day has an insatiable sweet tooth. Babe Ruth and Almond Joy were two of her favorite candy bars. She also loved Pepsi Colas.

Suffice it to say that she had a much heartier appetite than Jay. It goes without saying that we, children, joined in the snack fests.

As we grew older, Jay and Baby made sure that we understood the importance of learning and knowing about God. We attended Sunday school and church and accepted Christ as our Lord and Savior and were baptized at or around the age of twelve.

We learned very early that we had to be on our best behavior in church. It was extremely difficult at times to remain still without fidgeting, when we would be in church from nine o'clock until three o'clock; however, we knew better than to create a scene. I often thought that a school day was much easier. At least in school, we had recess and lunch.

As part of our spiritual growth, we learned many Bible verses which we then recited as our grace at the dinner table as well as in our Sunday school. We children liked Sunday school much better than church service but we anxiously looked forward to our church's activities including Easter programs and egg hunts, the Fourth of July picnics, when Granddad would always make homemade ice cream and serve it; and the Christmas programs.

We learned to share and to be responsible, contributing members of the family as we were required to participate in an assortment of chores around the house. These included making beds and helping wash the clothes. Before we got the washing machine, washing was a half day activity.

Washing clothes was done in a number ten size tin tub with a washing board. Water had to be drawn up in buckets to fill the tubs and pot; a fire had to be made around a large iron pot filled with water so that the white clothes could be boiled in order to whiten them. They were then taken out, rinsed and hung on a clothes line with clothes pins to dry. Colored clothes were washed and rinsed. When dry, the clothes were taken off the line and taken into the house. If old enough, we were required to iron.

Other home chores included sweeping the floors, washing dishes, mopping, sweeping the yard, feeding and milking the cows, feeding the chickens and hogs. E.D. and Willie also had to chop wood for the fireplace and stove and milk the cows. Diane and I would churn the milk and gather the butter. We were fascinated at the process of

If This Be Not Love

"sweet milk" changing its form, churning it, and getting delicious butter and buttermilk. As each child got old enough, he/she was taught to cook with the exception of the youngest son, Earl.

Garden and field chores included picking butter beans or peas and shelling them, blackberries, tomatoes and okra, peanuts from the plants after they had dried, chopping cotton, picking cotton, digging sweet and white potatoes from the ground, getting fresh ears of corn for dinners, then later gathering the corn for feed for the animals and cornmeal.

Going to the watermelon patch was always fun times. Other good times involved watching syrup being made. The sugar cane had to be put through a press which consisted of two large round iron cylinders about a foot in diameter and two feet tall that pressed the juices from the stalks of cane and funneled them into large vats. The press was designed so that an attachment could be tied to a mule that would go around in circles in order to turn the cylinders. A fire was then made underneath the vats to boil the juices. The juices were boiled until they thickened to a syrup consistency. We always found this activity fascinating and delighted in eating the rich, thick, syrup with hot buttered biscuits and home cured ham or bacon. We gathered fallen pecans from Granddad's pecan trees, and shelled peanuts so that Baby could roast them and make syrup candy/peanut brittles using our homemade syrup and homegrown peanuts.

Through the years, Christmas was always a wonderful time beginning with finding the "just right" tree on the land to finding red berries and holly and decorating for the season. Baby loved to bake during the holiday and prided herself on her chocolate and coconut layered cakes.

Licking the batter left on the spoon and in the mixing bowl was as great to us kids as eating the finished cake. There was always a battle as to who asked for the spoon or bowl first. The smells, tastes, and sounds of the Christmas seasons would linger in our memories. There was no TV but the radio would fill the house with the sounds of Christmas and we loved "Santa Claus is Coming to Town."

Jay and Baby made sure that each child got at least one toy and a goody bag filled with fruits, (apples, oranges, tangerines) nuts, (pecans, walnuts, Brazil nuts) and candies. The culminating events were the Christmas program at church and dinner.

Jay worked so much but those times he was home were great. As a young husband and father, his greatest joys came from providing for and being with his family. He taught the boys how to do those things he felt were male chores. He kept their hair cut; made sure the car and house were in good condition, mended fences, and with the help of the boys, chopped wood and tended to the livestock. He made time to take us for Sunday drives or to the community store for cones of ice cream or popsicles. We loved to huddle around him on the front porch as he would tell fantastic ghost stories.

Jay enjoyed listening to quartets sing spirituals on the radio on Sunday mornings as the family got ready for church and sang along. He also loved to "parch" peanuts on the stove or in the fireplace. Jay didn't roast chestnuts or marshmallows on the open fire but he did roast many, many peanuts. He would also put sweet potatoes into the ashes in the fireplace until they were soft. Then he would take them out, rinse, split and put homemade butter on them. They were delicious. If the potatoes were not sweet enough, he would add a little sugar.

Neither Jay nor Baby lamented about the lack of time to "do their thing," or to get away and relax because their focus was not on themselves but on providing for us. Jay took pride in being able to deliver when a request was made from us. He would give to us his last change and find someway of eking through to the next paycheck. His paycheck belonged to his family. It was not his to keep. Each week, he kept only enough money to buy gasoline for the car and a few dollars for emergencies.

The funeral continues. Cousin Jennifer is reading the tribute to Dad that I wrote and read to him while he was in the hospital.

WORDS OF EXPRESSION: AS A FATHER

DAD: The Rock of our Foundation

Dad, *because of you*
There are kindred spirits walking upright
Hearts filled with the love of Jesus.
Heads held high, living each day with an appreciation of life
A dedication to God for his love and grace
And a determination to live a life reflective of our model, you,
our earthly father, who set the standards by which we must live.
Dad, *because of you...*
Life is a challenge, positive, productive and good
Because of you
We have witnessed the depth and breadth of love and
dedication
Touch and influence the lives of many
Because of you
We know that the heart can overrule a drained and worn body
We have observed and marveled at your unlimited gift of giving
To God, to family, and to community
We have seen your willingness to reach out, to touch
To share, to support, and to encourage.
Dad, *Because of you*
Your children, grandchildren, and future generations
Will know the beauty of love, the essence of goodness, and the
value of an honest heart, an honest day's work, and an honest
effort to be positive contributing and productive human beings.
You are one of God's most precious creations.
He gave you to us for which we are grateful.
You have been and will always be our knight in shining armor
Although you have heard this so many times before
Please hear it again and know
We dearly love you
We respect and appreciate you for the Fine Person
Gentleman, Father, Provider, Supporter
Encourager, and Example that you have been for all of us.

WE LOVE YOU. WE LOVE YOU. WE LOVE YOU DAD

In 1951, Jay was able to buy his first new car, a Chevrolet. He, as well as the boys, were delighted and enjoyed the new acquisition fully. There were many joy rides for the family. Oftentimes during one of our rides, Baby would say, "I wonder where that road goes?"

Jay would respond, "You want to find out?"

Enthusiastically, Baby would answer, "Yes. Let's find out."

This led to many adventures and Baby especially, would find serenity and peace as she allowed the beauty of nature to embrace her.

Returning home from one of our outings, a rainstorm developed and heavy, blinding rains poured from the sky. Jay had a very difficult time seeing the road. There was no area on which he could pull off and I knew that there was a bridge over which we had to pass. I was terrified that we would drive off the road into the water. Fortunately, Jay was able to get us home safely. This fear and those brought about by other storms were the only fears that I had as a youngster that I felt was beyond my father's ability to relieve.

On January 30, 1952, Angela was born. Six weeks later on March 12, 1952, Mama Strong died at the age of seventy-seven. Before her death she gave to Baby her 18 carat gold wedding band. It would be the first time that Baby would wear a wedding ring and she continued to wear it until it literally wore through and fell from her finger.

Over the next two years, Jay and Baby would take Diane to a host of doctors and have her take a myriad of tests and examinations trying to find out what was causing her various symptoms. It would eventually be determined that she had leukemia.

WHEN DREAMS ARE TOSSED AND BLOWN

Experiencing much stress and unhappiness over their little girl's health condition, Jay and Baby looked forward with pride and anticipation to May of 1953 which would yield their first high school graduate. Edward, called E.D., was a good son and had been a good student. He had assumed the role of "man of the house" when Jay was away working in Gary. Although Baby, Willie and he ran the farm in Jay's absence, E.D. did not like farming.

He had a fun loving personality and was well liked by his buddies who called him "Po Jo" because of his tall and slender stature. In one of his many moments of teasing his siblings, and showing off what he had learned in school, he had said to Diane long before the doctors made a diagnosis, "Diane, You're so po; you look like your white corpuscles are eating up your red corpuscles." Little did he know that his statement was a true assessment of her condition.

On some Sunday mornings while Baby and Jay were getting the family ready for church, E.D. with Willie's help would catch a plump chicken from among the brood and wring its neck. They then plucked the feathers and prepared it for cooking. E.D., in order to have enough pieces, would cut it into ten pieces, with the liver, neck and gizzard as bonus pieces, season and fry it. In addition, he would make homemade biscuits, rice and gravy. This was one of the family's favorite breakfasts. Each family member had a favorite part of chicken and switching pieces was an option but seldom exercised and making a wish with the breastbone was an event.

Graduation for E.D. was approaching and senior fees were due which he was given. A few weeks before graduation, Eddie, Lee's oldest son and buddy to E.D., told his mother that Edward had joined the Army. Lee immediately told Baby. Jay and Baby were shocked, hurt and very disappointed. They confronted Edward and asked him, "Why E.D.? Why would you take your graduation fee money and go join the Army?"

Edward responded, "I don't want to plow a mule for the rest of my life."

Denied a long awaited privilege and celebration broke Baby's heart. She had plowed many days in order not to take the boys out of school to plow. She would stop plowing in time to make sure that there was a hot meal to eat after school and before our chores began. This was a crushing disappointment.

She did whatever she could to facilitate our doing well in school because school was always a priority to her. She had also liked his girlfriend and to emphasize the importance of remembering important days, she would buy a box of chocolate covered cherries and wrap them in pretty paper for him to give to her each Valentine's Day.

I remember this vividly because at that time, nobody could have convinced me that there was anything in the world that tasted better than those chocolate covered cherries. Baby would buy a second box and give each of us one. To have been the recipient of an entire box would have put me in my utopia. Time and old taste buds have brought about a change in that assessment. I look at them now and smile.

E.D. was sent to Okinawa, Japan. Willie then became "the man of the house" in Jay's absence. It was the dawning of new days for him who in the past had been living in the shadow of his brother. He had been rather sullen, argumentative, and negative. His new role

If This Be Not Love

provided him an opportunity to shine and shine he did. It brought about a brand new personality which manifested an unbelievable transformation in attitudes and behavior to the delight of the entire family.

In January of 1954, Diane, a beautiful frail little girl with beautiful eyes, long wavy hair, and an angelic personality had to be put into the hospital. She needed frequent transfusions of blood.

Shortly afterward, Jay spoke to Baby about a dream.

"Baby, Diane is not coming back home."

"Oh! Harris! Don't say that. I don't want to hear anything like that!"

"Baby, I had a dream and in that dream I saw two white doves in the corner of the room. One was large and one was small. I don't know who the large dove was but the little dove was Diane."

Her condition continued to worsen over the next months and the little girl who wanted so much to come home and go back to school and Sunday school died at age nine years nine months on March 24, 1954. Diane had wanted so much to get out of the hospital and be a part of the Easter Program at the church.

Several days passed. Baby, remembered the conversation with Jay about his dream of doves. "Harris, the large dove was Mama." Baby's mother had died two years earlier in the month of March.

Jay and Baby were deeply affected. Losing a child was something for which they had not nor could not prepare themselves. Neither had they prepared me, age eleven. I had lost my life long sister and companion. The next sister would now be six years my junior. We had often dressed alike and the funeral would be our final occasion. We wore matching satin white dresses.

She looked like a sleeping doll in the diminutive pink casket surrounded with a host of flowers. Her classmates, excused from school to attend the funeral, her teacher and community people filled the church.

Diane was buried in the church cemetery. She was the first of the immediate family to be placed there. There were flowers, so many flowers. Many came to the house. For years to come, Baby was not able to tolerate freshly cut flowers.

    Sandra, the ninth and last child was born on November 1, 1954. Jay and Baby were still having a hard time getting over Diane's death, but at this time it was Jay who was noticeably hurting. Baby suggested that the family move to Chicago as a means of getting his mind off Diane. Jay accepted the suggestion. She wrote and told Aunt Nellie of their plan. Aunt Nellie, who had no children and loved having children around, invited the family to come and stay with Uncle Bill and her in Benton Harbor, Michigan until the construction jobs opened up in the spring in Gary.

ON THE ROAD-STEP BY STEP

The second week of April 1955, the family of nine left Tuskegee, Alabama bound for Michigan in our 1951 Chevrolet. In preparation for the trip, Baby made a #10 size tub full of sandwiches, bought milk, cans of soda and placed bags of ice underneath them. Clothes were the only belongings taken. The car was very crowded but the only complaint was over who would sit next to the back windows. Three were in the front and five and a baby of five months were in the back. Willie helped Jay drive. The trip was made in fourteen/fifteen hours with no stops other than the gasoline/potty stops.

After arriving in Benton Harbor and getting settled in, Baby had the task of getting us enrolled in schools for the last seven weeks of the school term. She had brought with her updated report cards from our home schools. She had heard and knew that it was a practice of northern schools to put children arriving from the South back a grade.

Willie was in the eleventh grade. He, Earl and Linda were enrolled and placed in their respective grades without any controversy; however, I was in seventh grade and was to attend the "hardest" elementary school in the city. It was questionable whether the school would allow me to be placed in their seventh grade class. After deliberation and taking into consideration the report card of all A's, the counselor allowed the placement.

Baby was elated that all of us were placed into our right grades. She told anyone who would listen that, "The Lord blessed me with my children. It was by the grace of God that they were not put back a grade."

Getting my appropriate placement was easy compared to what I had to do to be able to pass to the eighth grade. Chapters and chapters of work had to be made up. After homework was completed, I had to spend several hours each night reading and studying materials in order to learn what had previously been taught. It was my first experience with stress.

Around the middle of May, Jay, Baby, and the three youngest children went to Aunt Lenora to stay until school was out. At the end of the school year in Michigan, all three of us passed to the next grade. Jay and Baby returned to pick us up. The family then moved into the basement apartment of Aunt Lenora's building on the west side of Chicago. Jay started his construction job the first of June.

The Pastor is enjoying telling the church about his visit to the house yesterday and the story about how Dad always looked out for Mother. He especially liked the one about Dad always making sure that the car was warm for her before she got into it during the winter months and the fact that she didn't have to ever put gas in any car. What the pastor does not know is that Dad warmed the car for his children as well.

The basement apartment had one bedroom, a living room, kitchen and bath. The living room doubled as a bedroom and family room. Hideaways sofas were bought to provide sleeping accommodations. All of the children slept in the living room area.

Willie returned to Tuskegee in the fall to complete his senior year of high school. He stayed with Granddad and Mama Lillie. Earl, Linda, Deborah and I were enrolled at Beidler Elementary School.

Baby was home for the first year. After Angela started kindergarten, Baby got a job at a plastic company making plastic kitchenware. She had Aunt Lenora keep Sandy. It became my responsibility to monitor my younger siblings after school making sure that they changed into play clothes, did homework, home chores and stayed out of trouble of any kind. Dinner had to be prepared and ready by the time Jay and Baby got home.

In May of 1956, Jay and Baby got to attend their first high school graduation. Willie graduated and returned to Chicago with them. It was not long after his arrival that he got a job with Sears, Roebuck and Company as a receiving clerk. After overcoming the hurdle in Michigan, I graduated from Beidler as the number one student in the class with perfect attendance and was the recipient of the American Legion Award. One of our graduation songs, "You'll Never Walk Alone" made a lasting impact on me and would often be remembered during tough times. It was a good year.

Between the years of 1957 and 1960, Jay continued to work in Gary. Baby was laid off from the plastic company. She then worked for the Chicago Transit Authority washing buses for several months and later worked at another plastic company making plastic bags. For a short time, she worked two jobs, a day shift at the plastic company and from seven to eleven at Speigel compiling zip codes of the various states.

During the summer of 1958, I told Baby that visiting Mama Lillie for the summer would make me "the happiest person in the world." Jay and Baby informed Mama Lillie and Granddad that I wanted to visit for the summer. They were happy to have all of us come down. I was sixteen and was finishing my sophomore year in high school. Earl was twelve; Linda was ten; Deborah was eight; Angela was six and Sandy was four. Shortly after school ended in June, Jay and Baby took us to Tuskegee.

Summer in Tuskegee did not turn out to be the dream summer vacation that I had imagined. Mama Lillie and Granddad were in the midst of harvesting and picking cotton. Shortly after arriving, all of us were helping to pick cotton. After breakfast, Mama Lillie and we would get our cotton sacks and head for the cotton field. Granddad would have already put in a couple of hours of picking before breakfast and he would return after breakfast ahead of the group.

It was not long after our arrival that while picking cotton I was bitten by an unseen insect that caused my fingers to turn purple and swell very badly. Screaming, I ran to Mama Lillie who sent me to the house to treat my fingers and hand. To the chagrin of my siblings, I did not go back into the fields for the remainder of the summer. I was later accused of faking lingering pain in the fingers and playing the role of a prima donna who strutted around carrying a parasol to shield the sun, while they were stuck picking cotton in the fields. What they failed to remember is that I was at the house cleaning or cooking meals for the family. Although they were not required to work everyday, my siblings' unpleasant memories of their times in the fields, of bites and stings, and skin reactions to pesticides were the only memories from that summer.

While we were in Tuskegee, Jay and Baby found a larger apartment on 15th Street. By the time the summer ended and we were picked up, Jay and Baby had settled into the apartment and were looking forward to enjoying the additional rooms.

At the end of August our parents drove to Tuskegee to pick us up. Upon arriving, Baby was horrified at the physical condition of Earl, Linda, Deborah and Angela. They had developed multiple sores on their arms and legs from bites and reactions to the pesticides. Sandy, the baby, and I had escaped because neither was in the fields for any period of time.

Once back in Chicago, Linda, Deborah and Angela had to be taken to the dermatologist several times before the sores cleared up. Linda's reactions had been the worst. Baby feared that she would have permanent scars on her legs from the opened lesions. Fortunately however, they healed without scaring. Baby vowed that she would never again allow her children to spend an extended period of time with anyone unless she accompanied them.

With the children back home, Jay and Baby quickly realized that the apartment was fine but existing situations, the neighborhood and the schools were not. The apartment was located on the third floor and often when coming up the stairs men would be sitting on the stairway and would hesitate to move or not move enough to allow comfortable passage. Their behavior made it extremely difficult to bring groceries or any bundle up the stairs; but more importantly,

Jay and Baby were concerned about their daughters having to pass these men daily.

Once we were enrolled in school and began to bring home the books and homework, Baby noticed that the assignments were lessons that had already been covered at our previous school. It was then that she knew that they had to find another place as quickly as possible. She solicited the help of Aunt Lenora and Cousin Portia.

Before the end of the first semester of school, Baby was told by Aunt Lenora that an apartment was available across the street from her building. Jay and Baby were fortunate in that through a slip up in management, they had not signed the lease and were under no obligations to remain in the apartment. The family was delighted to get out of that neighborhood and we were happy to get back to Beidler School. The family stayed at this location for a couple of years before moving to a large apartment up and across the street.

E.D. returned from the Army and was with the family for a short while before he left for New York.

In June of 1960, I graduated from John Marshall High School number seventeen of 276 students and was awarded for four years of perfect attendance. I was the first of five Marshall High graduates and elected to apply to the University of Illinois, Chicago campus at Navy Pier. I was accepted. Earl graduated elementary school.

The early sixties brought to Jay and Baby the joy of having their first child attend college along with the struggle to meet the added expenses. I had not gotten a scholarship and received only a small student loan. Baby got a job at Montgomery Ward which she would have for the next eleven years. Willie married Fannie. A year later in May of 1962, Willie's first son, Russell, was born.

HARD TIMES

Jay worked construction which was primarily seasonal with few jobs available during the harsh cold of winter in Illinois and Indiana. There were times when after completing a job he would apply for unemployment compensation while awaiting another job assignment. Although Jay and Baby had experienced hard times before making ends meet, it was at this time that things just seem to happen.

Jay was getting workman's compensation at sixty-five dollars a week and I, in my first year of college, needed about a hundred dollars for an immediate school need. They did not have all the money needed and although they had seldom borrowed money from friends or family, Baby felt that this situation merited an attempt. She contacted a brother who had no children, owned a two flat building and lived very well. Her sister-in-law answered the phone and she told her of the need for a loan of thirty-five to forty dollars and asked her to relay the information to her brother. She added that the loan would be for only a week and she would personally return the money.

If This Be Not Love

To Baby's dismay, her brother never called. She was however again rescued by Aunt Nellie, who wired the money and told Baby that she and Jay did not have to worry about paying it back. God had made a way.

Jay wanted for very few material things, and allowed himself few if any perks. Many times his coworkers would ask him to join them at a local bar to have a beer. He would invariably respond, "No man, I can't do that. I've got to go home, or I've got to take my daughters somewhere after school or pick them up." Jay would never allow his daughters to take public transportation at night.

After many attempts at trying to get Jay to go out with them, he eventually told his coworkers that he did not have money to spend on beer. "Man, what do you do with your money?"

"I have a daughter in college."

"Man, why are you wasting your money on a girl who is going to get married? Let her husband take care of her. You don't send girls to college for an education."

Jay responded, "Well, I'm sending mine so that they can get an education and not have to depend on any man to take care of them."

During these struggling times, Jay and Baby lost their new 1961 Star Chief Pontiac car. It was not unusual to be unable to find a parking space on the street where we lived. One day, the only near place to park was in the alley behind the apartment building. One of the neighborhood boys, about twelve years old, playing in the alley with other boys took the gas cap off our car and dropped a burning firecracker into the gas tank. The car exploded.

For Jay, this was a devastating event. His car was the only "toy" that he had. He found pleasure in his car whether it was old or new. A car not only provided reliable transportation for his family and for his getting to work, but it was a source of enjoyment for him.

As he watched flames destroy the car from our third floor back porch, he had to be physically restrained from going down to the alley. As a host of emotions engulfed him, tears spilled down his face.

Although the other boys had run away upon seeing what was about to occur, the culprit sustained burns. His parents lied and denied that he was the one that blew up the car. They claimed that he was an innocent victim and sued the insurance company.

With things going as they were, Jay and Baby were urged by some family members to apply for welfare which they had previously refused to do. With their financial situation showing no improvement, they eventually relented and made application. During the interview they were told that they could not have a telephone and that I had to come out of college and get a full time job. They completed the interview and application and as they left, they were told to call back in a couple of days.

Baby was mortified. There was no way that they were going to tell Harris and her what to do and how to run their family for a few dollars of assistance. When they got home from making application, the telephone had already been cut off. Baby called the phone company to inquire as to why the phone was off because she had paid the bill. She was told that the welfare office called and directed them to do so. Baby, finding it hard to keep her composure, spoke in a very deliberate and commanding voice. "My husband and I got this phone and we have paid each and every bill on time. Welfare has not given us one dime. We pay our bills and we expect you to turn our phone back on today." The phone was reconnected.

Furious at this action and the statement that I had to come out of school and work, Baby stated that she didn't and had never liked handouts and would not at this time start taking them. She had told the caseworker that I was working part-time at the University of Illinois Hospital as a clerk/typist but was told that was not good enough. Baby had no intentions of ever taking me out of school or of talking to the caseworker again.

Later the caseworker called and after being told that they were canceling the application, she wanted to know, "What about the children? How are you going to take care of them?"

Baby's response was, "We've taken care of them this far and we will continue to take care of them."

This determination to provide the very best that they could for us, had resulted in Jay and Baby's earlier refusal to live in public housing. They could have easily qualified for housing, but after visiting available units which were fairly new and very spacious, they decided against them even though their financial load would have been eased. Financial relief for Jay and Baby was not a consideration when it came at the expense of providing a more beneficial and safer environment for us.

WHEN THERE IS LOVE

During the majority of his working years, Jay did not remain unemployed for long periods of time. If not working his construction jobs, he was diligent in finding small jobs. Whether working his regular construction or other jobs, he was never too tired to spend quality time with his children. Oftentimes, after he had spent an exhausting day working and after having dinner, the younger girls would ask him to take them to the park. It was a request they did not make of Baby because they knew she was not a "park" person. Jay however, was never too tired and never refused them. This is something they loved and it would be talked about after they became adults and parents.

Although Baby was not a park person, it would be a park where she experienced one of her most frightening ventures as a mother. Jay and she had taken the four younger girls to Riverview Amusement Park in Chicago. Sandy, the baby, begged to go on a roller coaster ride. Baby tried to get Linda, Deborah, Angela, or Jay to ride with her but all said no. Not wanting to disappoint her baby and succumbing to a mother's love, she reluctantly agreed to take her on the ride.

Once the roller coaster started, Sandy began screaming "Mama, Mama." Wanting to scream but unable for fear of scaring Sandy more, Baby muted her terror but vowed that she would "never, ever, ever, get on one of those things again."

Baby continued making sure the younger children learned to be responsible and reliable too. Although the younger ones were growing up in the city rather than on a farm, there were still chores and an expected level of performance in whatever the task was, be it a home chore or an academic assignment. On several occasions, failure to bring home the correct change from a trip to the store for an item merited a return trip to correct the error. It did not matter if the shopper had been short changed a dollar or a penny. Baby expected the shopper to be able to know how much change he should have received to the penny and that a receipt was given. No excuses were accepted.

This level of performance was to be exhibited in school as well. She constantly monitored homework to assure that it was completed correctly and neatly. When there were tests, time was spent reviewing and she would quiz in preparation for the test. Therefore, when report card time came around, Baby expected A's and B's and would not sign a report card if there were other grades on it. Jay would have to sign.

As we grew up, Jay, for the most part, left disciplining the children to Baby, especially the girls. Both believed in "spare not the rod and spoil the child;" however, the stropping that we received were the results of tough love and making sure that we knew what behaviors were appropriate and acceptable as well as those not appropriate and would not be tolerated. All of us learned at an early age that there were consequences for unacceptable behavior.

Earl recalled that of the four or five whippings he received in growing up, the one he got for shooting a white kid with his home made slingshot was not merited. His friends and he had been playing in the alley with their slingshots that they had made. The hook of a wire hanger was used as the weapon. While in the alley Earl felt the rush of air from an object passing which barely missed his head. He looked down to find a brick lying near him. Looking up to see from where it came, he saw this kid standing on his back porch looking down at him. He then aimed his slingshot and sent the wire hook sailing toward his attacker. The boy was hit and let out a scream that could be heard throughout the neighborhood.

Earl received a whipping and at the time felt he was justified in what he did because he could have been killed or seriously injured had the brick hit his head. The old adage applied was that "two wrongs do not make a right."

Later Earl reflected on the event and said, "It was okay. It made up for the many other times that I should have gotten a whipping and I didn't."

Once the girls were old enough to date which was at the age of sixteen, Jay made it a point of meeting each young man and telling him what was expected of his behavior.

"You are taking my daughter out and I expect you to be a gentleman. If you don't, I have a shotgun that I keep loaded and I won't hesitate to use it."

The young men did not take this information lightly. We girls, not letting our date know, had many laughs and often joked about the looks that came over their faces and other effects that the warning produced.

The sixties was an eventful decade. In 1962, Linda graduated from elementary school and entered Marshall High School. She also became the owner of a piano in a rather creative manner. Because she had saved some money from doing odd jobs, she went shopping on Madison Street. She bought a guitar and had five dollars left. She then went to the store next door that sold pianos, saw one she liked and asked the salesman if she could put five dollars on it to hold until she brought her parents in to see it.

At dinner that night she told Jay and Baby that she had bought a piano and she wanted them to see it.

"How much did you pay for the piano Linda?"

"I put five dollars on it."

"How much does it cost?"

"Ohh, it's $300.00."

Jay and Baby went to see the piano and purchased it for their enterprising daughter even though they would have to make some financial adjustments.

1963, I was inducted into Delta Sigma Theta Sorority. I married William Michael Summers, a college classmate and football player who played in the 1963 Rose Bowl, in April of 1964 and graduated from the University of Illinois with a BA in Teaching of English with a Spanish minor in June of 1964. This was an event for the immediate family as well as the extended family because I was the first college graduate in the Harris/Strong family. I was later hired by the Champaign School District as a middle school English/Spanish teacher.

Earl graduated from Marshall High School number sixty-three of three hundred and thirteen graduates. Although he was on the track team, cross country team, junior concert band, orchestra, letterman's club, class representative and worked in the program office, he did maintain average grades. Deborah graduated elementary.

In the fall of 1964, Earl attended The University of Illinois at Navy Pier. He was in the last student body to attend the University at Navy Pier and in the first student body to attend the University at its new location, Circle Campus.

For Baby and Jay, this was a very good year except for the death of Baby's brother, Garrison, at age sixty. They were very proud of us and deservingly so. Both had labored, made many sacrifices and been steadfast in their devotion to our family throughout the years to get us to where we were. Their love, devotion and faith during hard times that God would "make a way out of no way" had prevailed. God continued to bless them and many of His blessings were seen through their children.

Baby wanted to see Niagara Falls and suggested to Jay that they go and take the younger children, Linda, Deborah, Angela and Sandra. Jay agreed. This was Jay and Baby's first vacation other than trips that they had made to visit family members. Baby was elated and awe struck by the sight of the Falls. Her reactions were tenfold to those of the children. She loved nature and the many wonders of the earth never ceased to amaze her.

The three days, two nights trip with a stop in Brooklyn, New York was an adventure that the family would remember and talk about for a long time. Other memorable family trips were the annual drives to Benton Harbor, Michigan during the fall when the foliage on the trees peaked in color. Getting away from the big city and its predominance of big buildings and cement, and visiting Aunt Nellie and Uncle Bill was a relaxing, yet invigorating experience that the entire family thoroughly enjoyed. Added to these sensations were the wonderful and delicious meals that Aunt Nellie prepared.

In June of 1965, my husband Michael graduated college; I finished my first year of teaching and we moved to Chicago. Michael Eric, our first son, was born December 14, 1965.

March 1966 Edward married Romie Jean Betts and in September 1966, Earl was drafted into the Army. He spent the majority of his two years in Viet Nam as a military policeman. Angela, the little genius, completed elementary school and became the last of the Marshall Commandos. Linda graduated high school number ninety-five of three hundred and seventy-five and entered Loop Jr. College which she attended for two years before transferring to Eastern Illinois University. Willie, having divorced Fannie, married Brenda. Yolanda was born September 22, 1966 on her grandfather's Jay's birthday, Sheldon, November 1969, and Diane, April 1972.

In 1967 Chicago was hit with the snowstorm of the century. Following unseasonably warm temperatures, snow began falling on Thursday morning, January 26 around five o'clock. It continued for the next twenty-four hours for an accumulation of twenty-three inches of snow with drifts as high as six feet.

For the next ten days, cold weather and more snow slowed the city. The Department of Streets and Sanitation estimated that 75 million tons of snow had fallen on Chicago. The majority of schools closed; however, in a few days the buses and trains were back running regularly although seldom on schedule. Baby was five minutes late to work one of those days and was docked pay. It was the first and only time during her tenure at Ward that she was late reporting to work. Jay was working on building a northern expressway. He was told not to report to work on Friday but work continued the next week as usual.

Children enjoyed the winter wonderland as never before. Beautiful snowmen were created and Florida children got to see some of the 75 million tons of snow. Rail cars were packed with snow and sent

If This Be Not Love

to Florida so children who had never experienced snow could romp and play in it.

About a month after the snowstorm of the century for Chicago, Craig, our second son, was born on March 29, 1967. A few months later, Edward and Jean became proud parents of Brian Edward on September 8, 1967. That December, Baby's father died at the age of 92.

1968 was a historical year for Chicago due to the Westside Riots following Dr. Martin Luther King's assassination in April and the National Democratic Convention in August. Deborah, Angela and Sandra experienced their schools being closed. I, then teaching, experienced my school closing after being shut down several days by noon because of a militant student group rioting through the halls. The culminating event before the school was closed occurred while there was a school assembly. Militant students went to the stage, picked the principal up as he sat in a chair and carried him out of the front door of the school. Businesses were also closed and many looted as fires enveloped the Westside. Rioting and rioters ran amok. Major Daley gave the infamous order to policemen. "Shoot looters on sight."

Glares from burning streets and smoke could be seen from the window of the apartment. For the first time, Jay and Baby found their family in the midst of a situation beyond their control. Although they were not political activists and were rather conservative in their views, the killing of King affected them. Nevertheless, they disapproved of the actions taken by the rioters and looters which were in direct contrast to the non-violence stand that King had championed. Angela shared with the family that Sammy Davis Jr. visited her school and encouraged the students not to get caught up in the violence

June 1968, Deborah graduated high school ranked number ten of eight hundred and fifty-six graduates and received an award for perfect attendance. The effect of the baby boomers on the enrollment at Marshall High School was apparent. The graduation class had jumped from 276 when I graduated in 1960 to a staggering 856 for Deborah. She matriculated to the University of Illinois, Chicago Circle Campus, where she completed a year before taking a year off.

After a year of working at the post office, experiencing earning good wages and enjoying the freedom of being an adult, Deborah was making no plans to return to school. Baby solicited my assistance in persuading and getting a reluctant Deborah to return. She entered Illinois State and received her BA degree in Teaching of English.

1968 Jay and Baby saw their last child complete elementary school. Sandra chose not to attend Marshall and took advantage of the first permissive transfer option and enrolled at Amundsen High School north of the city.

Jay and Baby had succeeded in getting the last of their eight children through elementary school which was a milestone. Earl returned home in July of 1968, a month before the horrors of the 1968 National Democratic Convention took place in downtown Chicago, having safely and successfully completed his tour of duty with the Army. The attacking of antiwar protesters by policemen was discussed not only because of its brutality, but because Earl had just returned from Viet Nam, the protested war.

By 1969 Jay and Baby were able to purchase their second home located south of the city on East 99th Street. They also proudly experienced seeing Edward and Willie become homeowners. I would buy a home a year later.

Angela graduated number four in her graduating class of over six hundred and entered Illinois Wesleyan University. She returned home for the summer after her first year having cut a foot of her hair off (much to the chagrin of Baby and me) and wore an "Angela Davis" afro to express Black Pride. Her dress oftentimes consisted of an army shirt, jeans and boots. She attended IWU for two years before transferring to the University of Chicago.

MORE FRUITS OF THEIR LABOR

The seventies was the decade of weddings, births of the majority of the grandchildren, career developments and/or improvements and the deaths of Granddad in 1974 and Mama Lillie in 1975.

Earl married Beverly Elmore March 6, 1970 on his 24th birthday and son Earl Jr. was born in October 1970. In 1971 he took courses at Control Data Institute for a year and received his diploma in Computer Technology. He then worked for Universal Oil Products, Cogna Systems, and CNA Insurance. In October 1974, Earl and Beverly bought their first home. He later accepted a position at the Corporate Office of McDonald's from which he would retire as a Systems Development Manager.

Deborah married David Wells, a college classmate, in September 1972, and began her career as a high school English teacher. Subsequently Kimberly was born in April of 1974; Tracy, August 1977 and David Earl IV, June 1986. David and she became homeowners in 1977.

Sandra interrupted her schooling and married Willie Lee in October 1972. Chrishonne was born in April of 1973; Willie Pervis, aka Butch, May 1976 and Tatiana, December 1985. Sandra enrolled in a nursing training program.

Linda received her BA in Sociology with a minor in Psychology in 1973. She received her Masters in Education in 1974 as well as married a college classmate, Sandy Osei-Agyeman, in June 1974. He, an Olympic runner, had run in 1972 in West Germany but was denied the opportunity to run in Canada in 1976 because his country, Ghana, along with other African countries withdrew from the Olympics as a means of protesting apartheid in South Africa. Linda was hired by Bethany Hospital and worked in the Drug Abuse Program before taking a job with AllState. Idris was born November 1976 and Deborah Iyana, July 1984. May of 1984, Linda and Sandy bought their first home. Linda would eventually retire from AllState as Systems Director of Billing.

Angela received her Bachelor of Arts degree in Psychology in 1973 from the University of Chicago. She married Frank Walker, a Dartmouth graduate, in April of 1977 and they stayed with Jay and Baby a few months until they had saved enough to make a down payment on a home. Their house was purchased in the autumn of 1977. Tina was born December 1978. Angela received her Masters of Business Administration with a concentration in Human Resources from the University of Chicago in August 1980 and Veronica, aka Nikki, was born November 1980. She was employed by IBM before taking a job at Georgia State University in Placement. She would eventually take the position of Acting Director of Career Services.

I worked towards my Masters degree while teaching and received it in Education, Administration/Supervision in May 1977. I would retire from education as a principal.

Jay and Baby enjoyed their home on the south side of Chicago. They found a church and attended regularly. Baby, although working steadily, had to see the doctor because her heart tended to flutter wildly at times. After examining her, the doctor queried as to her home life and if Harris and the children were treating her well. Baby assured him that there was nothing happening in her life that she felt would attribute to her heart condition. Her relationship with Harris and her children was fine. He then recommended that she see a psychiatrist which baffled Baby. She returned home and spoke to Jay.

"Harris, the doctor says that he wants to send me to see a psychiatrist. I thought psychiatrists were for crazy people. What do you think?"

"Baby, I don't know."

That night Baby dreamed. *Diane approached the room where she was sleeping from a long hallway. She had been in the room at the end of the hallway.*

"Mutt Dear. I can't go back to sleep. I can't go back to sleep Mutt Dear."

"Okay baby, I'll come and lie down with you." Baby stays with Diane until she falls asleep.

The next morning Diane awakes. "I'm all right Mutt Dear. I'm all right. You don't have to worry about me. Don't worry about me."

After waking up Baby told Jay, "Harris, I don't have to see a psychiatrist. The Lord showed me what has been bothering me in my dream. It was Diane." She then told him of the dream. Baby also remembered how throughout the years, she had occasionally found herself totally unfocused. Whatever she would have been looking for would actually be right in front of her and she would not see it. She had found that there were times when she did not function well but could not pinpoint the cause.

After the dream, Baby continued to take medication for her heart; however, she now realized that part of her problem was that she had not gotten over Diane's death. Once realizing this, she was able to face the problem. It was only then that the emotions and the lingering effects of Diane's death started to wane.

Jay voiced that he wanted to work until he was 65. Baby convinced him, that at age 62, he had been burned enough by the cold of winters and the heat of summers to retire. He did not need to subject himself to that for another three years.

"When I retire Baby, I want to go back home."

"Harris, we can't move back home. I've been with these children since I was seventeen years old. We wouldn't be able to eat because of the phone bill."

"Okay, okay Baby."

The next morning Jay got up and got ready to go to church.

"Baby, are you going to church?"

"I don't think so Harris."

Jay went to church and Baby stayed home. During his absence she said, "Something came over me." She thought of how hard Jay had worked throughout all the years they had been together and all that he had sacrificed for his family. She did not want to deny him his wish. She smiled as she remembered some of the good times that they had shared throughout the years. Then she realized that she could leave the children and return to Tuskegee with her husband and be just fine.

As a young couple, they had left Tuskegee in order to provide a better life for their family. They could at this time look at their children and know that they had done the very best that they could do. Jay and Baby had often said that "God had made a way out of no way." Each of their children was now functioning as a positive, productive citizen of which they could be proud. Some had done better than others. Some had stumbled along the way, but stumbles were used as building blocks. Most importantly, none of their children had gotten lost. They readily counted their blessings.

When Jay returned from church, Baby told him about the feelings that she had experienced. "Harris, you know what. I can leave these children. I can go to Tuskegee."

"Oh, that's good Baby. I'm so happy to hear you say that."

THE RETURN

Jay and Baby decided that they wanted their new home to sit on the highest point of the land. This would be about a hundred yards east of the original home site, closer to the main road which allowed them a northern overlook of the adjoining property. Jay wanted to build a brick, three-bedroom and two-bathroom home.

At the same time, Aunt Nellie, now a widow had made the decision to move to Tuskegee. She was in the process of looking at trailer homes. Baby accompanied her on one of her searches and "fell in love" with one of the modular homes that she saw. It had three bedrooms, two baths with a huge family room with a beam ceiling, and a separate dining room. More importantly, the difference in cost of the two homes would be over $30,000. She collected brochures.

The majority of us wanted and encouraged Jay to build his brick home. We offered to provide financial support if a time or circumstance deemed it necessary. Angela and Earl however, talked to mother and brought up some points that caused her to lean even farther towards the modular home. They stated that Jay and Baby were in their retirement years, and as much as they wanted to travel, they would not want to be tied down with heavy financial obligations.

Baby had listened to the pledges of support from us but she knew that Jay and she would not place themselves in a situation where they would have to rely on their children. After the talk with Angela and Earl, Baby showed Jay the brochures of the modular home. They discussed the pros and cons of each house and the difference in the cost. Jay liked the modular home and told Baby although it had cedar siding, it could be "bricked up" later.

"Okay Baby." Baby put in the order.

Moving Jay and Baby back to Tuskegee was a family affair. The largest U Haul truck was rented and everyone pitched in to get things packed and loaded carefully so no damage would be sustained. Willie supervised while Earl and David, Deborah's husband, did the packing of the truck. We finished packing around 10:00 P.M. and those making the trek to Tuskegee sought needed rest and sleep for the night on mattresses on the floor of the home that was now sold. The rest of us returned to our homes.

This was a bittersweet time for us. We would miss their presence; being able to run over to visit at will; inviting them at the last moment to come over for dinner, or to see a new home acquisition; telling them that we are coming over and that we wanted to eat some good collard greens; having babysitting service and a host of other things. The house now owned by others was the place where Deborah was married; where there was a party to celebrate three college graduates: Linda, Deborah and Angela; where grandson Michael Eric, at age four, told his grandmother after she had reprimanded him, "Mama Lolis, you talk rough!"

The sweet was that our parents deserved whatever they desired and we all wanted them to be happy. They had given so much to us, primarily a solid foundation on which to build our lives. We did not wear the big brand name clothes, nor were we showered with unnecessary material things that we didn't need. We were however, acknowledged for our successes. Graduation parties were given; supplemental purchases included spring dresses, bonnets, and prom gowns. I attended three proms during high school. The younger ones had pet birds. Family fun times included Easter eggs hunts conducted

If This Be Not Love

in the apartment, trips made to Garfield Park Conservatory, museums, parks, amusement parks, and joy rides. These fun times were enjoyed by all, but what we were given most and what had the most effective and lasting influence in our lives were the love, security, constant guidance, and Christian values that we received.

This momentous time for the family found eight adult children, seven, with whom Jay and Baby over twenty years earlier had traveled north, assisting them in their return to the homeland. Their quest had been to provide a better life for these children, and by the grace of God, they had fulfilled their mission.

They could now return home with a feeling of contentment and pride yet humble, for they knew Proverbs 16:3 - states that "In his heart a man plans his course but the Lord determines his steps;" and Proverbs 19:21- "Many are plans in a man's heart but it is the Lord's purpose that prevail." So with thanksgiving in their hearts, they were going back home to be together and alone for the first time in forty-two years.

At 3:00 A.M. the next morning, the Harris caravan headed to Tuskegee. Edward and Earl shared driving the U Haul while Linda drove Mother's car with Sandra's daughter Chris, and Baby as passengers. Jay drove his car with his grandson Butch, Sandra's son and Sandra, as passengers.

Upon arriving in Tuskegee, Jay was elated to be back on the land that he loved and knew so well. Getting settled took several months but once completed, he and Mother got back to their gardening. The garden yielded a bountiful crop that Jay and Baby were more than willing to share; however, they found that oftentimes neighbors were quite willing to accept the free produce from the garden if they had harvested them, but not interested if they had to harvest for themselves.

Within three years Jay and Baby had amassed enough bricks to have the house bricked up. They hired a bricklayer for eleven hundred dollars to do the job. Jay finally had his brick house and he was delighted.

The minister's eulogy is winding down. It was good with interjections of humor. Dad would have enjoyed it.

In 1982 Jay was ordained as a deacon at Midway. He and Baby started out on another of life's missions. They found themselves involved almost daily in caretaking a family member or neighbor. Over the next ten years, Jay would not only attend to matters within the church but assumed the responsibility of making sure that the church cemetery was maintained.

He and Baby were also concerned about the lack of access to the church by wheelchair and for elderly people who found stairs hard to negotiate and would build a much needed ramp. Jay's skills used in construction were exercised as he and Baby undertook the job. They were the ones to go to the adjoining towns looking for improved lighting for the church and would be the decision makers on the selection and purchase.

In August of 1982, Jay and Baby had to bury their second child. Edward, their first born, four month before his forty-seventh birthday, died of liver cancer. Throughout his illness, E.D. maintained a positive attitude and played golf when he literally had to be carried around the golf course. His sense of humor was refreshing and uplifting in his final days.

In his hospital room he stated, "I don't want anyone crying over me because I have lived and enjoyed my life. I also enjoyed running my insurance agency." He jokingly said, "I can see it now. All those folks will be looking down at me in the casket and I will look better than all of them." He was a handsome fellow.

It was again difficult for Jay and Baby to bury yet another child; however, because of their growth and development as individuals and especially as Christians, they were stronger and able to cope better this time. This was also the year that Baby's brother "Shorty," one of the "three musketeers" died.

Jay and Baby were treated by their children to a trip to the Bahamas for their 50th anniversary celebration in 1985. It was the

If This Be Not Love

first time that they would leave the United States. Linda and her husband accompanied them.

Throughout their marriage, Jay had made looking out for his Baby a priority. He didn't just provide for her. He was her protector. He did everything within his ability to make sure that no harm came to Baby. He was ever aware of things that could possibly bring harm to her and would warn her ahead of time.

While in the Bahamas the four went out walking. Linda found that Jay was constantly looking at the walkway. Taking Baby's arm, he said, "Watch out Baby. There are a lot of big cracks and breaks in this pavement."

Upon hearing this, Linda bantered, "My gosh, Dad. You're treating that woman as if she's some kind of queen!"

Jay looked directly into Linda's eyes and retorted, "Linda, she is my queen."

Those words left Linda speechless.

This behavior was not unlike the countless other times when he would warn Baby to step back from a car when visitors were pulling off, or be careful using that knife or watch out for that. He was forever very watchful of his wife and family. Baby told of a trip going through the mountains of Tennessee when she had told Jay to let her drive to relieve him.

It was dusk when she took over driving. Jay took the passenger seat while the girls in the back seat slept. After driving for a while, Baby noticed that a car approached from behind. When she would speed up, it would speed up and when she slowed, it slowed. Jay was not very visible in his sleeping position. Baby thought that Jay was asleep and kept driving and said nothing.

She did not know that he was well aware of what was happening. "Baby, when you get to an area where you can pull over, pull over. Those guys are up to no good."

Shortly afterward, Baby pulled over and the car passed. Jay took over driving. He had not driven very far before they came upon the same car which had stopped. Two white men were at the back of it with the trunk opened, one on each side of the trunk. Jay passed. He was not tailed.

Willie and his wife, Sylvia, took them on a road trip that included Disney World in the late eighties. Baby was finally getting to travel more, her long awaited dream.

Michael Eric, my son, would be Jay and Baby's first grandchild to finish college. In 1987, he graduated from Northwestern University in Chicago with a Bachelor of Arts. He would later enter Northwestern School of Law and receive his Juris Doctor degree in 1990. Craig Alan, my second son, would be the second grandchild to complete college. Graduating from Union College in Schenectady, New York, he received awards for *Highest Character and Meritorious Service* from Union College faculty. They would set the educational bars for their generation.

Jay and Baby lost two other family members in the eighties, Jay's sister Louise in 1988 at the age of 71 and in 1989, David, an older brother of Mother, at the age of 91.

The pear trees and small grape arbor that Jay and Baby had planted were now producing. Baby enjoyed making pear preserves, and canning pears for future pies. She had not lost her touch from her younger years. She also began to bake fruit cakes during the Christmas season to give to each of the children. She had found a recipe for making a pineapple casserole and it had become the dessert dish that we would "engage in battle" over. Sweet potato pies were stables but came in second to the pineapple casserole.

Maintaining the grounds around the house was a huge task. Jay bought a riding lawn mower to cut the acre of land that surrounded the house. He loved it but it was a challenge for Baby to keep him from mowing down her flowers in the yard or whacking off parts of special bushes.

The backyard was plugged by them, a bit at a time, with St. Augustine grass which developed into a plush lawn and functioned well at stopping washes from the flow of water that occurred when there was a heavy rain. The grass in the front yard did not grow as well because of large maple and pine trees; however, coverage was finally attained. Baby then planted several crepe myrtles, a magnolia tree and other decorative plants and flowers. It had been a challenge for them, but when all was done, the bricked up modular home, sitting

If This Be Not Love

on an acre of land with its huge lawn, garden, and small fruit arbor looked like a small resort surrounded by groves of pine trees.

This was the land that had been purchased forty-eight years earlier. For Jay and Baby, the journey leading up to this time in their life had been a long but blessed and productive one. From the front porch they could see the chimney standing as a monument to their first home. It was a reminder of how far they had come. Life together began there in 1935 in their two-room house, later expanded into a four-room house, with an outdoor toilet. At this time, the eighties, they were exceedingly happy with three bedrooms and two full baths.

More important to them was their state of health. Both were feeling great and had energy to do whatever they wanted to do within reason. They retired each day with smiles and hearts filled with thanksgiving.

From the dining room bay window, the view was serene. It overlooked the front yard with its bird bath and the road to the house, with a back drop of cedar trees on the other side. Having a meal in this room with Jay and Baby in this setting was always a very special occasion for all of us children who also felt that the food served, be it breakfast, lunch or dinner was always a culinary treat. Jay did not eat as well as Baby thought he should; but, "Just let one of his kids come to visit and his appetite explodes."

There was something very special about the way Baby seasoned her food. There were some items we didn't cook, such as ox tails, which we loved even though we realized that they certainly would not be found in the Lean Cuisine section. Her smothered chicken, country fried steak with onions, banana puddings, fresh fried corn, pound cakes, and even rutabagas were mouth watering good. Baby learned later in life how to cook tasty rutabagas. When we were children, we all hated them because she would cook them with salt pork and only add salt and pepper.

Although Jay was now 75 and Baby was 72, they were able to be "providers" for family members and neighbors. When they were not providing their time in order to fulfill an assortment of needs, they were called upon to provide transportation to the doctor, hospital, to pay monthly bills "up town," or to the grocery store. Family members and neighbors knew that they could be relied upon. Their faith was made complete by what they did. "You see that a person is justified by what he does and not by faith alone." James 2:24

1992 was the year that the women in the family along with Deborah's mother-in-law, Olivia, and sister-in-law, Barbara, declared independence and took a cruise to the Bahamas leaving the men behind. Each husband upon learning of the trip had his own "I can't believe it" reaction.

"You're doing what?"

"You've got to be kidding."

"What am I going to eat?"

Willie came down and stayed with Jay. Baby unlike the rest of the women prepared meals and placed them in the freezer.

Baby would enjoy her first cruise and was the one of the eight women traveling who got the most attention from the cruise attendants. The rest of us couldn't figure out what she had that we didn't, so we swallowed our pride, grinned and contented ourselves being observers.

Between 1990 and 1996, Baby would lose four of her sisters. Aunt Nellie, whom she took into her home for a period of time before her death, died at age 79 in 1990. At age 72, the caretaking job was more than Baby and Jay, age 75, should have undertaken. It was a physical strain on both and caused some health problems. Aunt Lenora died in August of 1992 at age 87; Aunt Johnnie Mae in January of 1996, age 89, and Aunt Georgia in November of 1996 at age 87. With the passing of these four, only Aunt Emma Lee and Baby, the two youngest of the Freeman/Strong family remained.

In 1992, Jay began to experience getting tired very easily. He and Baby cut down on the amount of gardening. This condition continued along with his feeling cold often. He began to go through a series of tests to determine the source of his problems.

Marie, Jay's baby sister who lived in Detroit for the majority of her life, died in October 1994 at the age of 72.

Jay and Baby's 60th wedding anniversary, January 1995, found him in the hospital in Alabama suffering from negative reactions to medication given during testing. The doctors had concluded that his heart was causing his conditions. All the children, as well as some of our mates, took the party to his hospital room. He was in good spirits and Baby told stories of their early life.

Jay returned home. His positive demeanor and humor were still intact. In the summer of '95, Sandra recalled an occasion while she was staying with Jay and Baby. She was wearing a breezy, sleeveless blouse tucked into khaki shorts. (She admitted to having put on a few extra pounds.) Jay entered the house and noticed what she was wearing. He walked over to her, gave her a big hug and said to no one in particular.

"This is my baby." He then looked her over from head to toe. "My BIG Baby."

We all had a big laugh on hearing this story but I was reminded that this was one of two areas in which I heard Baby criticize Jay to us. She felt that he had a tendency to say the wrong thing to people in regards to weight. Upon meeting a friend or family member that he had not seen for a while, and if he/she had gained noticeably weight, Jay would say with a big smile while shaking their hands or giving them a hug, "Well, I can see that you have not been missing any meals." Baby would just roll her eyes at him.

The other area was the speed that he drove at times after returning to Tuskegee. Previously, Baby was okay with Jay's driving, but felt at his age, his reflexes were not good enough to handle any situation caused by speed.

Over the next year, he was not sick nor did he suffer from aches or pains. He was concerned about his heart and he continued to experience coldness; however, it did not hinder him from assisting Baby in the care of Aunt Georgia who was ailing and needed care. As with Aunt Nellie, Baby and Jay were the primary caretakers who maintained constant contact and took care of any needs that Aunt Georgia may have had. Aunt Emma also helped out when she could. Aunt Georgia would later tell Baby that she was going into a nursing home because the care needed was too much for Jay, Aunt Emma, and her.

In May of 1996, Earl and Beverly took Jay and Baby to see the Grand Canyon. Their trip took them through Mississippi, Louisiana with an overnight stay in Dallas, and El Paso. They continued to Tucson, Phoenix, and finally arrived in Flagstaff where they did another overnight. After spending a day at the Canyons, the travelers spent another night in Flagstaff before leaving for Albuquerque, New Mexico.

On the return trip, they traveled through Amarillo, Texas, Oklahoma City, Little Rock, Arkansas, then Birmingham, and Montgomery, Alabama before arriving in Tuskegee.

It was a dream vacation for Baby and Jay. They felt as if they could not adequately describe the joy that had been experienced while visiting the Grand Canyon and the various states. Baby, the daredevil of the two, had oftentimes ventured too far out on a ledge or stood too close to something that warranted a "watch out Baby" from her protector, Jay. She was experiencing what she had dreamed of and wanted from childhood and shied away from very little.

Later in 1996, Baby had a dream in which she saw that "Harris would be on me." I called the same day that Baby had the dream and was told about it. I, who had moved to Roswell, Georgia told her that "Jay being on her" did not have to happen and invited them to come and live with my husband Alex and me. I also wanted to get Jay with a reputable heart specialist and have him treated in one of the best hospitals.

They did not sell as I suggested but packed up some of their belongings and drove to Roswell. They would be spending the majority of their time in Roswell and would be going home occasionally between Jay's treatments.

Jay was taken to a doctor affiliated with St. Joseph Hospital. He was told that he did not have heart disease after extensive testing was done. During this time he spent several weeks in the hospital. It was finally concluded that he was suffering from the lack of blood due to multiple myeloma, which accounted for his tiredness and feeling cold. Words can not describe my feelings when I realized what multiple myeloma was and that my dad, Jay, was suffering from it. He would be the third family member in our family to be diagnosed with a type of cancer. We had already lost Diane and Edward.

At the time Jay was in the hospital, Sandra was working a nursing shift from 7 A.M. to 7 P.M. She remembered that on one long and grueling day, having eaten only cafeteria food, she, still in her uniform went to visit Jay. After greeting Baby and her sisters, she leaned over to kiss Jay and asked how he was feeling. With a bright smile, despite any discomfort, he responded that he was feeling okay. Then he asked, "Sandy?"

"Yeah, Daddy?"

"Do you have any toothpaste at home?"

Baffled by this question, I answered, "Yeah, Daddy."

He looked me straight in the eyes. "Do you use it?"

"This was said with a straight face. Sometimes Daddy's straight forwardness was only exceeded by his sense of humor."

During the summer of 1997, Jay remained upbeat and active. While I was planting a Leyland Cypress in the back yard, he made sure from his chair on the patio with his sharp eyes and keen sense of balance that the tree was set perfectly straight. I would later call it Daddy's tree. He also was well enough to take a trip with Baby and me to Chicago to see his grandson's, Michael Eric who was now a practicing attorney, new home.

Shortly after returning, Jay's need for transfusions of blood and platelets increased and as the cancer worsened, he had to be transfused as often as five times a week. He received chemotherapy as well as several radiation treatments to the left side of his head where the cancer had localized and was causing severe pain.

Jay handled his condition well during this period. This was the first time in his life that he had been afflicted with a crippling medical condition. He had never been sick with anything more serious than the flu and he was baffled as to where this multiple myeloma came from and why. The doctors and nurses liked him and were excellent. Their warm and caring demeanors as well as their expertise eased a very trying period of time for Jay and us. Jay continued to be a pleasant person with humor which made the job of taking care of him so much easier.

He was six feet two inches tall with a thirty-two inch waist. His neck was a size 16. Jay was a dapper dresser and his daughters frequently told him after he had dressed for an occasion in a suit, shirt and tie that he looked as if he'd just stepped out of *GQ Magazine.* He would also smell great in his after shave or cologne. I was vigilant in keeping him at this time well shaven and wearing a pleasant after shave.

After a long day at the cancer center, Baby and I would return home weary and wonder what we could cook quickly that would be pleasing as well. It was Jay who often came up with suggestions and none would include buttermilk. Happy to get these suggestions, Baby or I would prepare the suggested meal which would be one that neither of us would have thought to cook.

There was a very short period of time when Jay weakened and it was difficult getting him up the stairs. Baby and Jay were again offered our bedroom on the main level but Baby was determined that they would not take it. This weakness lasted but a few days and Baby gave credit to God answering her prayers. She said that she had prayed continuously asking Him to strengthen Jay so that he would be able to walk up the stairs. Her prayers were answered. He, in his weakened condition, and at age 82, walked up the stairs to the second level until he left for Tuskegee. I would walk behind him with my hand in the small of his back to assure that he would not fall backward.

Jay's brother, Oscar, who had served as a policeman in Cleveland was buried the second week in October 1997 at the age of 78. Jay was unable to attend the funeral but Willie and Earl went to represent the family. Jay now was the lone survivor of the Gordon/Harris family. Within a couple of weeks, he and Baby decided to return home. It had become apparent that Jay would not survive the cancer. He wanted to go home.

After arriving in Tuskegee, Jay remained at home for about a week before he was placed in the hospital. He would spend his final three weeks there. Family members took turns spending time with him, both days and nights. Church members, and neighbors visited and he was always a gracious patient. He would put on a happy face and enjoyed each visit in spite of his pain.

Alex and I had booked a cruise to the Bahamas for the Thanksgiving weekend several months earlier. I visited Jay and told him that I would be back in a couple of days and to be good and make sure he was there when I returned. It was however; a promise he could not keep. Jay died the day that Alex and I left from Florida on the cruise. Notification of his death was awaiting me when I arrived at our lodging in the Bahamas.

Stricken with grief, I tried desperately to find immediate transportation back to the States. It was difficult to say the least. Upon making contact with the family, I was told that it was not necessary to make the emergency trip. The family was working together to make funeral arrangements.

I had spent the last year with Jay and Baby and could not help but feel cheated. I had been with him for so much of the time but lost the chance to say good-bye. My cry was "Dad, how could you do this to me?" I was going to be gone just a couple of days!"

The final song "I made it" is dedicated and sung by the pastor.

Final Thoughts
I have finished now with this house of clay
Please kindly and carefully lay it away
And let me rest from this life of pain
Toiling in sunshine, storm, and rain
Trying to help the sick and poor
And turning no needy from my door
I strived to do my master's work
Never a duty did I shirk
Many times I was misunderstood
When I had done the best I could
I am tired now, so let me rest
Don't cry, don't you know God knows best
Please, no sad hearts, no hung down heads
Don't weep for me for I am not dead
I have another house you know
Where only God's redeemed can go
I do not need this house of clay
So tenderly, carefully, lay it away
(Author unknown)

There are no tears for we have given tribute and recognition to one of the finest human beings I have ever known. His life was one of giving and sharing. He was truly a selfless, caring, loving husband, father, and friend. I frequently marveled at his patience and his ability to take on others and help care for them. He did not retire. Yes, he retired from the everyday eight to four-thirty job. It was however, replaced with a twenty-four seven on call service for family and the community. After working a lifetime to provide and protect his family, he did not waiver when his Baby asked for his help in caring for two of her terminally ill sisters, one when he was 75 and another at 81. He was at her side willing to do whatever was needed. There were times when I thought his providing transportation for the community was just too much. He didn't. He epitomized "love thy neighbor as thyself," as well as Dr. Martin Luther King's exhortation:

"Everybody can be great, because everybody can serve. You don't have to have a college degree to serve. You don't have to have to make your subject and your verb agree to serve. You don't have to know about Plato and Aristotle to serve. You don't have to know Einstein's "Theory of Relativity" to serve. You don't have to know the Second Theory of Thermal Dynamics in Physics to serve. You only need a heart full of grace, a soul generated by love, and you can be that servant." Excerpt from the sermon "The Drum Major Instinct."

He was a Christian defined by his deeds; words were inadequate. He was indeed a servant for his family and community and this consistent dedication was not an afterthought, nor was it something that he did after he had fulfilled his cup, but it was his life, a life of sacrificing and giving. His physical presence will be missed so much, but that spirit of his will be with each and every one of us forever. His smile and humor will cheer us on cloudy days; his strength and tenacity will be remembered and help us to overcome setbacks or obstacles; his ability to give will be there to remind us of what's really important in this life, as we go forward and attempt to emulate the Christian life that he so well modeled for us.

"Let us not become weary in doing good, for at the proper time we will reap a harvest if we do not give up. Therefore as we have opportunity, let us do good to all people, especially to those who belong to the family of believers. Galatians 6: 9-10

BABY

Baby was now alone in her home for the first time in her life. She had gone from her father's house to her inlaws' house, to her home with Jay. Now she was faced with living in her home without Harris. Not only was there a sense of loneliness but there was fear. Baby found that she was afraid especially at night to be alone. She had been prepared for Harris' death by her special mode of communication with God. He had through a dream shown her that he would leave her.

Baby dreaming: *She and Harris start walking to church. They are on their private dirt road that leads to the main road. She looks back to the house and wonders, why are we walking when we have two cars? Halfway to the main road a vine from the shoulder of the road catches and wraps around her legs. She falls to the ground and the right side of her face hits the ground. She lifts her head and looks up. She sees Harris quite a distance away. She cries out, "Harris, Help me. Help me!" Harris keeps walking as if he didn't hear her. She thinks: I got to get up from here. Cars come down this road and I'll get run over. She struggles and finally gets free. She's* mystified and upset with Harris. "Why didn't Harris stop and help me? This has never happen before. He has never refused to help me. He's always been there for me." Baby gets free and continues to the main road, then up the road to the church. As she approaches the church, she sees Harris standing by the front stairs of the church. She decides to get back at him for not helping her by pretending not to see him. Baby wakes up.

As in her previous dreams, Baby felt that God was making her aware of a crucial situation that was occurring or about to occur in her life. In that dream, He was preparing her for Harris' death. She had and was handling the loss well but not the fear of being alone.

Baby could have easily opted to live with one of her children, but at this time she chose to remain in Tuskegee citing often that she did not want to leave her home, her church, or that she enjoyed the independence and ability to go wherever she wanted because she knew her surroundings. She could drive and feel comfortable in Tuskegee because she did not have to deal with high volume traffic. She knew the town and adjacent towns and often drove to them to shop.

Although she was comfortable, Baby had to deal with her fear. She went to the best source she knew, God. She began praying a specific pray for God to remove her fear and she prayed daily. She also talked to her pastor.

Within a short period of time, Baby had another dream. *An unknown man, Lee and she were in a car driving through a very desolate area. There was nothing to be seen on this long and winding road and it seemed as if it had not been used for years. They came upon an old shabby restaurant and stopped, got out and went in. They found there was nothing inside. As they walked around, they discovered there were two rooms, a front and a back door. Lee said to them. "I heard that two men in a car are driving around and shooting people. Let's get out of here." She and the man went through one door and Baby went through another. When she came out her door, she saw a very high mountain right across the street and Lee and the man were climbing up. Baby crossed the street and began to climb but after she had gotten about halfway, her knee began to ache very badly and she stopped climbing. She hoped that when the two got to the top that they would find a way of helping her; however, when she looked up again, the two had disappeared but she was at the top of the mountain.* To Baby, the message was: Others will leave you but "I am with you always." (Matthew 28:20) It was not long before Baby rested comfortably at night and was not afraid.

She was elated and told friends and family that she did not fear any more for she felt that God would not let anyone come into her house and harm her. Joyfully, she related her experience to her sister.

"Lois, you should not go around telling people this because there are people out there who may come in on you just to prove you wrong."

"Lee, don't you know that God is above all. If God does not want anyone to come in on me, no one will come in on me!"

Baby's faith was unshakeable. She had put her safety in God's hands and did not waiver.

In a subsequent dream: *Baby is in bed when she sees a very short male figure, about three feet tall, come up on the front porch through her bedroom window. He enters the house and comes directly to her bedroom and stands beside her bed. Behind him, stands a much taller male figure that just appeared. Baby did not see him enter the room.*

As the short one hovers over her bed, Baby yells at him. "I'm not afraid of you! Get out of my house! Get out of my house! My life belongs to my Lord and Savior, Jesus Christ. I don't want you or need you in my life." He disappeared immediately as well as the taller figure.

Baby interpreted her dream as proof that Her Lord would always be her protector. The short figure, Satan, had tried to instill the fear that God had removed. But Baby was not shaken by his appearance. The taller figure, a protector sent by God, was further assurance for her.

In January of 1998, Baby's 80th birthday party was taken to her. Children, as well as sister, nieces, nephews and friends gathered in Tuskegee for the occasion. It was a gala affair that found Baby full of energy and feeling fine. She ate heartily and was a real southern belle as she showed off or modeled her various gifts. She loved all of them but the framed collage of her family with her mother, father, sisters and brothers was priceless. It was given to her by niece Lessie, Aunt Johnnie Mae's daughter. As we watched Baby during the afternoon enjoying family and friends, we verbalized our hopes of being in such great physical condition and having her mental acuity at the age of eighty.

She remained in Tuskegee until late summer when she moved back to my house in Roswell to undergo medical treatment. Her right leg had begun to swell and she was having problems with her right hip, but as a whole Baby was as she said "in pretty good health."

While accompanying Debbie and me on a trip to Pike's Nursery, Baby became dizzy and sank to the floor. She was in sight of Debbie, who upon seeing this screamed "Margie! Margie!"

As I rushed to her, I asked the clerks to call for the paramedics. She was taken to St. Joseph Hospital. The diagnosis was heart disease. Baby's heart was too weak and beating so slowly that one of the paramedics had stated that he was surprised that she had survived the ride to the hospital.

Baby was given an angioplasty because of severe clogging of her artery. She later was told that she needed a pacemaker to regulate the beat of her heart. She received the news and did not hesitate to accept either of the procedures. There was a period of adjustment to the pacemaker, but once it was fine tuned to her heart, all was well.

Baby accompanied me to my church which is also Debbie and David's church. It is a large Church of Christ. For all of her life she had been a participant in a small Baptist Church and she missed that intimate environment. She had been an active deacon's wife as well as a Sunday school teacher and she loved both roles. She wanted to find a similar church.

Fortunately, such a church existed a few blocks from the house in the heart of Roswell. I took her to Pleasant Hill Baptist Church. After her first visit, she decided that it was the church that she wanted to attend. She had thoroughly enjoyed the service. It was a small church, and within a comfortable driving distance. Baby had basically given up driving because she felt that Georgia drivers drove as if they were on a race track. She would often say, "I'm too old and

If This Be Not Love

my nerves just can't take it." When she did not feel up to driving, a church member would pick her up.

A few months after Baby had received her pacemaker, she was told that she needed a hip replacement. Undaunted at facing such surgery, she, at age 80, gave thumbs up to the procedure. Her family was amazed at how bravely she accepted each of the needed procedures.

The healing process from the hip replacement surgery went very well. She spent her initial recuperative time in David and Deborah's home. There she was on the first floor without putting anyone out of a bedroom. They converted their study/library into a bedroom for her. Baby experienced very little discomfort. The worse side effect was the soreness in her arms from having to raise her body with the stirrups while in the hospital after the surgery. Throughout each of her procedures, she had remained basically independent.

Several months after recovering from the hip surgery, she was ready to go back home to Tuskegee. Over protests from us that she was at an age where she should be with someone, Baby opted to leave Roswell. I teasingly referred to her as the bionic woman who had gotten all of her parts fixed and was now ready to take on the world again. The fact that she was "eighty plus" didn't matter. She could not wait to get back in her house and back in an environment where she could drive to where ever she wanted to go, whenever she wanted to go. She also wanted to get back to her Sunday school class where she had not only enjoyed teaching but enjoyed the preparation leading up to teaching the class.

Baby would spend hours reading the Bible and the Sunday school book, making notations on cross references, as well as reading the Concordia. She would look up any word that she did not fully understand and consult with one of her children as to the correct pronunciation of it if she were not sure. She enjoyed teaching and she missed doing it.

Her class members had constantly complimented her on doing a fantastic job of explaining the lesson as well as her persistence in getting each member actively involved. Baby wanted her class back. The stay in Roswell had been good and she was truly thankful for being blessed with such attentive children; however, she was well now and it was time to go home.

Once back, Baby had to adjust to living alone and being totally on her own again. There were days when she really missed being around her kids but her loneliness was not enough to make her want to change her living arrangement. We, children, kept in contact on a daily basis and Deborah and I helped her to decorate the place to her liking. Even though Baby felt perfectly safe and that God would protect her from harm, Earl put in a security system. Each of the children was concerned about Baby being alone because times had changed in Tuskegee and there was an element of danger existing.

Caretaking of the grounds had to be given over to a lawn service. Baby still found plenty to do on the outside. The fruit arbor continued to produce fruit which she would gather and can, or make preserves. She also began making fruit cakes for each of her children for the Christmas Holiday.

In August of 2000, Earl and Beverly took Baby on a tour of the New England states. On this trip she would travel from Naperville, Illinois through Indiana, Ohio, and spend a night in Danville, Pennsylvania before arriving in New York City where she viewed the Statue of Liberty and the World Headquarters of Jehovah's Witnesses. From there they traveled to Danbury, Connecticut for an overnight stay at Hilton Hotel Towers. After breakfast, there was a tour of the Watchtower Educational Center in Paterson, New York and later a tour of Watchtower Farms in Wallkill, New York.

Returning to the Hilton for the night, the travelers would have breakfast the next morning before heading north through Waterbury and Hartford, Connecticut; Worcester, Massachusetts, Portsmouth, New Hampshire and Portland, Maine before arriving in Bangor, Maine. Here Baby would order her first whole lobster. When she was told that she was expected to eat the "whole thing" Baby responded, "I'm not eating that." She gladly settled for what she was accustomed to, the tail.

If This Be Not Love

After leaving Bangor the next morning, she was taken for a tour of Acadia National Park before leaving for Marlboro, Massachusetts for a three day stay. While staying in Marlboro, the first driving tour included Worcester, and Leominster, Massachusetts, Brattleboro, and White River Junction, Vermont; Lebanon, Manchester and Nashua, New Hampshire; and Lowell, Massachusetts. The following day, Tuesday, the tour included Boston, Plymouth Rock, and Cape Cod. On Wednesday, the day was spent touring Martha's Vineyard.

After leaving Marlboro, the route would take them through Providence, Rhode Island, New London, New Haven, Bridgeport and Stanford, Connecticut; New York, Bronx, and Patterson, New Jersey before arriving again in Danville, Pennsylvania for an overnight before heading home to Naperville.

Baby had for the third time traveled to and through places that she had only dreamed of visiting. The trips to the Bahamas and the Grand Canyon and now the East Coast were all intended to help fulfill her dream but more so to honor very deserving parents.

Returning home, Mother had many stories to tell about her trip. She loved going to places that she had read about or had seen on television. She had said to Earl while traveling that she questioned how people could see the many magnificent creations in nature and witness the various phenomena on earth and not believe that there was a God.

The most amusing story was her speaking of her reaction to seeing Plymouth Rock. I had already told Earl how disappointed I was when I saw the historic rock, but Earl did not tell Baby. She, as did I, had always envisioned a grand site with a prominent elevation. To both our chagrin, the small rock encircled by a protector rope like fence was a huge disappointment.

In 2002, I celebrated my sixtieth birthday by having a formal party in my home for the family. Baby was beautiful in her formal attire as well as all my sisters. The men, some in tuxedoes, were quite dapper. Michael, my son the attorney, who loves cooking provided us with a gourmet meal. It was a wonderful fun filled event that would be remembered.

Little did any of us know at the time, but our youngest sister, Sandra, who danced away the evening, would soon be diagnosed with a very rare cancer that was found in her knee. She would undergo knee surgery and chemotherapy. She suffered greatly from the chemo and refused treatment after taking half of the prescribed treatments. The chemo administered was too strong and was virtually destroying her body.

After stopping the chemo treatments, she went to see her primary physician who informed her that if she had not stopped the treatments, they would have killed her. Her heart had slowed to an abnormal pace. God saved Sandra and today she is cancer free. Her walking gait shows little if any signs of the knee surgery.

Continuing his quest to fulfill Baby's dreams of travel, Earl booked an Alaskan cruise. His wife, Beverly, Baby and I joined him for the eight-day, seven-night cruise which departed from Seattle, Washington July 19, 2003. He invited me to join them so that Baby would have a companion in her cabin. Baby was enthralled with the sights that allowed her to see nature unlike any that she had seen before.

All day Sunday and early Monday morning we were at sea. The ship entered Chatham Strait which took us to the Keku Island Pilot Station. After the pilot boarded, the ship turned into Frederick's Sound which led to Stephen's Passage, which is located between the Brothers and Sisters Islands, and past the majestic Taku Glacier in Taku inlet. It then sailed into Gastineau Channel where the capital city of Juneau is located.

After taking a tender to shore, we toured the Mendenhall Glacier Valley and learned about glaciers, their movements and the effects they create as they move. As we viewed the glacier, Baby was surprised that the temperature was as mild as it was in a valley of ice.

Tuesday was spent cruising Glacier Bay and we arrived in Sitka, Alaska on Wednesday morning. We again took tender service to shore and toured Sitka's National Historic Park and the Alaska Raptor's Center whose mission is to rehabilitate injured bald eagles and other birds of prey, educate the public and conduct bald eagle research. Seeing these magnificent birds up close was a wonderful experience.

Leaving Sitka, the ship entered the Alexander Archipelago at Cape Ommanney, and turned into Sumner Strait at Cape Decision which led to snow passage west of Zarembo Island ending up in Clarence Strait. At Guard Island we turned into Tongrass Narrows and headed for Ketchikan.

On Thursday, we arrived in Ketchikan, Alaska, known as Alaska's first city, which was established in 1887 when a salmon cannery was built at the mouth of Ketchikan Creek. Seeing salmon in mass numbers was awesome. We were also mesmerized by the "Stories in Cedar" featuring the great story tellers, the totem poles, many standing as much as two stories tall. It was a day of seeing mixed cultures offering wonders and inspiration. Dancers, doing dances of Russia entertained us not only with their skill in dancing but showcased the country's dress and offered a glimpse of its culture. Baby took a picture with two Russian attired dancers. Later we enjoyed shopping for souvenirs.

After departing Ketchikan at 1:00 P.M. on Thursday, we were at sea until 6:00 P.M. on Friday at which time we arrived in Victoria, British Columbia Canada. We took a short tour of Victoria and visited the John Stanley Plaskett Center to see his historic telescope. At midnight we departed Victoria for Seattle. Passing through the Puget Sound, we arrived in Seattle at 6:25 A.M. on Saturday morning after having enjoyed a vacation to be remembered for a lifetime.

Although Baby, 85 years of age, had undergone hip replacement surgery and had received a pacemaker, she continued to be blessed with a relatively strong and healthy body. Her hearing loss was and is at times frustrating but with the assistance of a hearing aid, she is handling it to the best of her ability. Baby experienced no ills on the cruise and no health issue kept her from participating in any of the activities of the group. She did not think twice about doing the walking tours and several were taken. She also enjoyed dressing for dinner and dining each day.

Baby returned home energized and happy. For the next six months she would continue to live in Tuskegee. She, continuing in the tradition that Jay and she had paved, took "under wing" a niece who suffered from sickle cell anemia and lived several miles away with her three children. She did not have any means of transportation and often called Baby to take her various places. She accommodated her niece but had to tell her that all trips had to be made during daylight hours. Baby did not see well doing night driving nor did she like being out at night.

As time passed, Baby began to feel the need to be closer to her children. She had four daughters now living in the Atlanta area, and one moving to Georgia, who had been urging her to move there. Although she had entertained the thought, she did not want to give up her independence. I offered to add a mother-in-law wing onto the house, but she wanted to maintain a place where at any time, any of her children and their spouses could come "home" and be comfortable during their visit.

Slowly however, Baby accepted the fact that she needed to leave Tuskegee. This meant that she would have to sell the place that had been home to her for almost seventy years. Although Jay and she left for periods of time, they always returned to where their roots were so firmly embedded. It would not be easy to give up "home." Furthermore, putting the house on the market meant that people would be traipsing through her home over a period of time and she did not want to be bothered.

Understanding not only her feelings, but also concerned for her safety during the time the house would be on the market, I decided to purchase the home to prevent her from going through this ordeal. In March of 2004, the purchased was completed. In the meantime, Baby, with the assistance of all her daughters, had looked and found a house for her just five minutes from Linda, who had recently moved to Georgia from Oak Park, Illinois. It was a cute white house with dark green shutters, three bedrooms and two baths that backed up to a golf course. Although Baby was accustomed to far more land around her, she felt that she could and would be able to adapt.

A couple of days after the sale of her home in Tuskegee, Baby, with the assistance of Linda, paid cash for her home in Georgia. Several days later, her family would assist her in moving from Tuskegee to her new residence.

Although the furniture was in place and the house organized, it would be some time before Baby would feel "at home" in this house, for she had left in Tuskegee a life that was the culmination of her growth from childhood. Once settled, she experienced something that she had never experienced before.

If This Be Not Love

Although we, children, had pitched in and gotten her situated, had added decorations here and there, and attended to any need that she may have had, she felt no real interest in the home. She moved through the days basically in what she felt was "a robotic state" never revealing to any of us how she was really feeling. It was only after she found herself "coming out of this fog" did she talk about what she had gone through. Because she was not treated for this condition, we could only speculate that perhaps she had suffered from a form of depression.

She gradually regained energy that she felt was gone forever. She began to find projects in and outside the house that she could do or wanted to have done. Baby felt good and was happy to leave that segment of her life behind.

It was through the grace of God that she had been blessed with good neighbors, Marsha and James, who came and welcomed her into the neighborhood. They also invited her to their church, First Baptist Church of Jonesboro, and told her that they would provide transportation. Baby had already attended two other churches but was still searching for a church home. She was very appreciative and took them up on their offer which led her to the church that she would elect to attend.

Although a large church, Baby enjoyed the Bible classes and the services immensely. In addition, she could attend church services and hear the entire sermon because of the earphones provided. She enthusiastically spoke of how much she enjoyed attending and was grateful to Marsha who saw to it that she got her earphones each Sunday. Her inability to hear well had been a source of frustration at Midway because she oftentimes missed many parts of the sermons or presentations of speakers. Now, she was hearing ninety-five percent of the sermons. After several months, she moved her membership.

Baby has had hearing aids for years; however, they are inadequate in compensating for the hearing loss. She suffers from nerve deafness and the amplification of sounds helps only marginally. Participating in her Bible class is limited now because of this and it bothers her.

She would love to be more vocal and active in the discussions but she has resigned herself that she will attend and participate to the best of her ability.

I attribute her satisfying church experiences, the constant attention of her family, and her new church family with helping her to get beyond that debilitating stage in her life.

Strength and perseverance in her faith have taken her as well as her family through many obstacles and unfortunate times and blessings continue to flow. One of her most recent was the finding that her daughter Angela, who was diagnosed in 2005 as having ovarian cancer, was now cancer-free and enjoying some of the best times of her life.

2005 ended with Baby, age 87, happy and contented. She is not on any prescribed medication and experiences few pains. She doesn't like and does not take any medication. She does take several natural herbs to address her occasional pains or discomforts. She celebrated her 88th birthday on January 12, 2006 and can still outwork most of her daughters. We tell her that we don't want her around when we are cleaning because she out cleans and out lasts all of us. None of us want her in our kitchens because unlike hers, our pots don't look like they just came out of the box. So rather than being embarrassed by finding her scrubbing them, or tending to other imperfections in our kitchens, we shoo her away.

It was just recently that she stopped out walking us when we go to the malls but she can still out figure most of her children. We rely on calculators. She has always "figured in her head." Baby acknowledges that she has been truly blessed with a beautiful life. Jay and her life was far from the bed of roses that so many of us wish for but seldom attain; yet through all the hard times my parents did not fail to "look to the Lord." "We also rejoice in our sufferings, because we know that suffering produces perseverance, perseverance, character, and character hope." Romans 5:3 and though Jay, Edward, and Diane died of cancer, Sandra as well as Angela are now cancer free. We as a family give thanks to God and continue to nurture our relationship with Him. We, children, feel exceedingly blessed and thank Him for allowing us to have Jay and Baby as our parents.

Their roots are in Tuskegee. It was in and around this city that they were born, played, schooled, married, birthed all of their children except one, and lived off and on our twenty acres of land for a period of over eighty-six years. Jay is buried in Midway Baptist Church's cemetery along with son, Edward, daughter, Diane and other family members. There are many ties that bind and Baby has every intention of eventually returning there. Her final resting place will be alongside her friend and dear husband Harris. To assure this, she has already made the arrangements.

EPILOGUE

Jimmie Lois Strong Harris was the baby of twelve. How would others describe her? People all around often spoke of a beauty that she never saw. Jay referred to her as his "brown-skinned beauty" and felt that she was pretty whether dressed in tattered work clothing with unkempt hair or dressed to perfection. She was the "apple of his eye." On the other hand, Baby never felt that she "looked good in anything."

In her earlier years, her natural curly hair was often straightened to the chagrin of Jay. Although she was a size six/eight when she married, she would wear sizes ranging from twelve to fourteen in order to get an appropriate length for her five feet eight inch stature. She was a tall girl in her day and could not find clothing long enough. Her weight would increase and stabilize at size twelve. During those times when she felt that she had gained too much weight, Jay never saw it. "Baby, you look good," was often spoken and not meant as flattery but exemplified how he saw her.

Baby and Jay grew up with us. She and Jay married as teenagers and had to learn how to cope with outside negative influences and circumstances and not allow anything to come between them and their love for each other and their children. As teenagers and young adults, they struggled with self-development as individuals while making a living, making ends meet and raising nine children. Baby followed some of the rules handed down to her from her mother relative to children. She and Jay came up with their own.

As a young mother, Baby had to be strong physically as well as mentally and emotionally; however, she encountered situations that caused her to rely on her steadfast faith in God to help her through or overcome. One was her deep-seated fear of dark clouds steaming from her childhood. The sight of dark clouds would cause her to "get so scared that I would tremble." When Baby was going through this, we as children did not sense the fear.

Preparation for a storm was very regimented. Depending on the time of day, certain tasks had to be performed; however, in all situations, the windows and doors had to be secured, the electricity turned off and we would sit together quietly until the storm was over. The storms would come with very strong winds that would literally shake the house and lightening bolts could be heard striking different areas. The pounding of the rain on the tin roof would be deafening. We were frightened by these storms but we never knew or sensed Baby's fear.

Similarly, we were kept out of the conflict that she was having with our grandmother. She could have easily turned us against Mama Lillie given all the negative things that she did; yet my siblings are only now as they read the book, discovering the many ugly ways of our grandmother.

As I end the story of Jay and Baby, March, 2006, Baby is doing very well after having to have her pacemaker replaced on January 27. She remains in basically good health and the only medication taken is an occasional aspirin or Tylenol. As before, she faced bravely a situation in which her life was threatened. This time it was due to the possibility of an infected heart and the removal of the stints from the infected heart that could have resulted in her bleeding to death. Her pacemaker had eroded (broken through her skin) leaving an opened lesion susceptible to an infection. By the grace of God, no infection was found. She then opted for a procedure that did not entail the removal of the stints, just the removal and replacement of the old pacemaker.

With several of her family members in her room after returning from surgery, Baby talked and visited with us as if she were at home hosting a family gathering. I was amazed and relayed to her how I'd never seen anyone come out from under anesthesia so quickly and be so alert. She simply smiled.

In April 1997, Baby decided to write some things down about her life. The following pages have been included because they are invaluable. Baby, at age 88, is no longer able to write well because of tremors in her hands; however, I have always admired her handwriting and her ability to express herself. These unedited pages will allow the readers to meet Baby "up close and personally."

Today is April 16, 1997. On January 17, 1997 I was 79 years old. By the grace of God, I am blessed with good health.

My name is Jimmie Lois Strong Harris, the youngest of twelve (12) children born to Willie Lue Freeman Strong and George W. Strong. There was eight girls and four boys.

I thank God for Christian parents. We was brought up and taught well with love and respect for all man kind.

We lived in the beautiful country. We were farmers. We planted cotton, corn, sugar cane, millet, peas, okra, collards, turnips, cabbages, mustard, onions, shellots, lima beans, pole beans, string beans, sweet potatoes, white and red potatoes and every thing else my mother could think of.

There was cows, mules, hogs, chickens, dogs and cats. We shelled corn with our hands and our father would take it to the grist-meal and have it grounded into meal, also grits.

There was fruit trees. Also figs. I loved canning season, and syrup making and buying things.

There was lots of blackberries. We picked them and canned them. There was a man for several years would come out in the country and ask people to pick berries and sell them to him. We picked many gallons and sold them to him for twenty (20) cents per gallon. That was in the 1920est.

There was no radios or telephones out in our part of the country.

There was enjoyable times to be had. We had communities base ball clubs, Churches and Schools. We played base ball at school during lunch hour, and other games. Schools would give Concerts and all the Communities would look forward to that.

Our Parents were very strict. We all ways had to be home before sundown. When my older sisters wanted to go to a ball game they would tell me to ask our father. We couldn't go no place without his permission. Even when we asked our Mother she would give her permission but would all ways say "ask your father." He was strictly the head of the home.

With the school being less than 1/4 mile from our home and all of my sisters and brothers that was still at home was in school, "it went only thru 6th grade", I would get lonesome at home. I was only 3 years old. My mother would let me go to school for a few hours. The teachers lived with us during school terms. Mrs Coprich was my favorite one. She would let me sit with the premier class. I learned as much as the older ones there. Being so young I would miss

My mother and start crying, and the Teacher would tell me I could go home after she found out the reason I was crying. Sometimes I would go to the school twice a day. Oh how I loved school. ~~I was~~ After growing older I would read everything I could get my hands on, which wasn't very much. Our father all ways bought all of our school books and there was all ways a dictionary in our home. There was no library we could use, except miles away at Tuskegee Normal school, which years later was named Tuskegee Institute, which name now is Tuskegee University. But I would read my books over and over. I wanted to be a Math Teacher. Math and history was my favorite subjects. My father wasn't able to send me to high school. I went three (3) months in the seventh (7th) grade. Oh how much I learned from those books. I attended Lewis Adams school on the campus of Tuskegee untill one of my older sister who was a nurse for a white family in Tuskegee who I was living with moved to Opelika, so that was it for me. My oldest brother lived in Chicago, Il. and he and his wife asked my father to let me come and stay with them and go to school. Also a preacher cousin who lived in West ~~Virgon~~ Virgina of my father and his wife asked my father to let me come and stay with them and they also would send me to school. But my father said he couldn't let his "baby" leave them. So o o d I missed my education. It was only two(2) years ago I stopped dreaming of being in school.

None of my sisters or brothers went to high school. They all had a good primer thro 6th grade education. They all married at age 18 (the girls) except me. I was still wanting to go to school. They knew they wasn't going. So we was having a wedding at our home every 2 years. The girls was two years older than each other. So the community got accost um to a strong girl wedding every 2 years. Oh the cakes pies and food they would cook up. The house smelled much like Christmas. The marriages and receptions was all done at home. The brides would be so beautiful in the white dresses my mother had made for them. She was a good seamstress. She made all of our clothes.

Me I met my boy friend thro his sister. She told him there was a baby faced girl in Lewis Cedar school with long wavy hair and could talk history and really good in math. I was 14 when I was in Lewis Adams, one year later my sister 2 years older than me boy friend asked this cousin of his to come with him to see his girl friend's sister

So he did. This was a tall handsome young man so he says fell in love with me on first sight. After dating for a while he asked me to marry him, I told him I was too young to marry. I still was wanting to go to school, I was only 16.

~~One day later he comes he and his father to~~ My sister got married and I went to visit her and my father told me I could spend a week with her. While I was at my sister," my ~~brother in~~ law, and my boy friend lived within calling distant" He and his father went to my ~~home and~~ asked my father for me.

My father told him as he did all the men that asked for his daughters not to hit me, they had raised me and if we couldn't get along to bring me back home. He also told him to bring me home the next day from my sister.

~~When my boy~~ He sent his mother to my sister to tell me that my father said for him to bring me home. She also told me he had asked for me. The reason for his father going with him my father was a deacon and his was also.

When my boy friend came to pick me up to take me home and as we were on our way he was telling me how much he loved me and what he wanted to give me. I told him I didn't want him. He started slowing the car down and looking funny and asking me did I mean it. I was all ways a scarry cat. Being the youngest of the ~~big~~ large family I was all ways protected. I was alone then and I was afraid I never could express my self to my father. So I said I was teasing. He was satified then. I really wasn't teasing. I wasn't ready for marriage. When we got home and he left, my father told me what had been said. They even had set the date, or rather he did. This was the middle of the week and he set the date for that saturday which was the 5th day of January 1935 One week before I would have been 17. I couldn't tell my parents I didn't want to marry. Oh how I wanted to. This guy was as nice as any one could be. My parents liked him. He would all ways found time to talk with them. I enjoyed being with him but I didn't want to marry.

~~Of course he take his parents to their party~~ He went to get the marriage license. He was 19 years old. His father was with him. But when he told how old I was he was told one of my parents would have to sign. He came to our home and told my father. My father went with him to sign. Oh if I could have told my father not to sign. I was very bashful in my young ~~life~~ life.

~~On~~ January 5, 1935 he taken his parents to their

pastor's house and came to our home to pick us up. We were married at 2 P.M. That saturday was a beautiful sunny day.

I really didn't like married life. He was so good to me. He never knew I didn't like being married. For years I was still a spoiled brat. If I was angry or couldn't get my way I would pout.

After three children the Lord showed me my life with him and I was ashamed of myself. On our eighth, or a week before our eighth anniversary I said, next week is our eighth anniversary. He said, that long? I said yes. I said if I ask you something will you tell me the truth? He said yes. Oh yes after seeing myself how selfish I had been to him I changed to be an unselfish wife. I still didn't tell him how ugly I had been to him and how the Lord showed me. Anyway I asked him out of the eight years we had been married which ones have been the happiest to him the first 6 or the last 2. The last 2 is when I had changed. He said you want the truth, I said yes. He said, these last 2 years you have been as sweet as a "grass hopper with a pie jumper on." One of his cute sayings. I was so glad to hear him say that. He said the first years wasn't as good. I asked him how could he stay with me. He said he knew I was my parents baby and he knew I was young and spoiled and he just prayed and asked God's help. Oh I wasn't a hell raiser, just pout. I am thankful that he didn't give up on wanting me for a wife and putting up with my selfish ways for a while.

We are the parents of 9 beautiful children Six girls and three boys.

Did I ever name my friend? His name is Willie J. Harris. He is an over average good husband and father. We have had 62 happy and wonderful years together. He will be 82 years old on September 22, 1997. A very wise young man at age 19.

ABOUT THE AUTHOR

Margie Summers-Gladney was born in Tuskegee, Alabama in 1942. She received her AB in English in 1964 and Master of Education Degree in Administration/Supervision in 1977, both from the University of Illinois. She spent twenty-three years in the Chicago School System beginning as an English teacher and serving as a curriculum coordinator/staff development, counselor, and assistant principal.

She was principal of Woodland Elementary School in Hazel Crest, Illinois from 1991 to 1994.

Prior writings include an in-depth study entitled "The Black Student's Perception of the Black Teacher" lauded by her professor as publishable material and "My Special Guest," a published poem. She has edited two published books.

Margie is the proud mother of two sons: Michael, an attorney, and Craig, a community developer. She presently resides in Roswell, Georgia with husband Alex and enjoys being a mentor for her church Atlanta Outreach Program, bowling, crafts, and crossword puzzles.

Printed in the United States
71267LV00004B/38